THE GRUMPUS

AND HIS
DASTARDLY, DREADFUL
CHRISTMAS PLAN

Translated from the original North Polish by

Alex T. Smith

An illustrated Christmas chapter book
for children and, of course, Grumpuses

MACMILLAN CHILDREN'S BOOKS

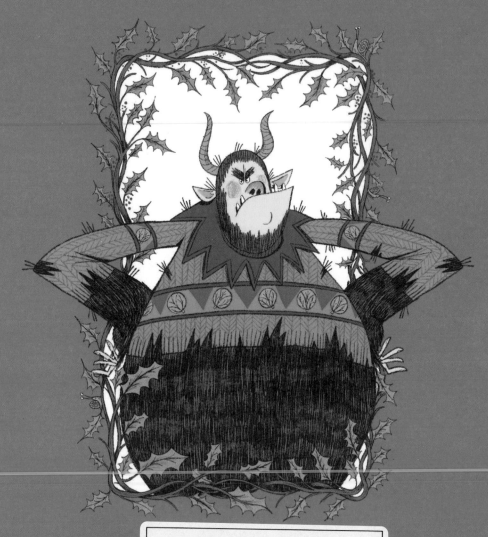

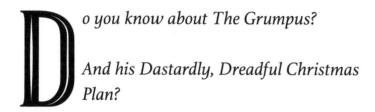

o you know about The Grumpus?

And his Dastardly, Dreadful Christmas Plan?

And about the Awful Thing that happened on Christmas Eve?

Perhaps I should tell you about it . . .

Of course, it really starts with a creak and a crack and a splintering, and a great wibble and a wobble . . .

But I'll tell you more about that later.

Instead, let's begin our story miles away from THAT disaster, in a tiny hodge-podge of a town where everyone has woken up fizzing with excitement.

Well, almost everyone has . . .

I'll give you one guess who HASN'T . . .

CHAPTER 1

IN WHICH THERE ARE SOME GLUM THOUGHTS THOUGHT ABOUT WHILST SCRATCHING

Once upon a winter's morning, The Grumpus stood in the door of his house, scratching his armpit with a –

HANG ON.

Do you know who The Grumpus is?

No, I don't suppose you do – there is only one of them after all, and not enough people know about him. And they should because of what he did – well, we'll get to that bit later on . . .

I think I should maybe tell you all about him first before we start our story properly. OK?

OK.

Right, well, pretend you haven't read any of this and now turn the page and we'll start again.

CHAPTER 1
(AGAIN)

IN WHICH WE START AGAIN AND YOU ARE PROPERLY INTRODUCED TO A VERY UNUSUAL CREATURE

Have you heard of The Grumpus?

No, I don't suppose you have, until now, because there is only one Grumpus in the whole world. His name is actually Theodore Grumpus. The Grumpus for short. Capital T for The and capital G for Grumpus.

The Grumpus is a large, hairy creature with long arms, short legs, sticky-out ears, pointy horns and big feet that he often trips over, much to his annoyance.

He lives in a small, wonky town, in a small, wonky house surrounded by high hedges and a heavy gate. There is a sign on the gate that says KEEP OUT! with no 'please' after it. The Grumpus lives there all by himself, which is just the way he likes it, THANK YOU VERY MUCH.

You see, The Grumpus is actually a big, grumbly, huffy-puffy, pinch-the-bridge-of-your-nose-and-sigh-loudly-like-a-sat-upon-whoopee-cushion, grumpy grump of a creature who doesn't like anybody. AT ALL.

In fact, The Grumpus doesn't like (hardly) ANYTHING. And if you don't believe me, just turn the page.

CHAPTER 2

In Which Several Of The Things The Grumpus Does Not Like At All Are Listed

- Being hot
- Being cold
- Being tired
- Being hungry
- Mornings
- Afternoons
- Evenings
- Bedtime
- Scrambled eggs
- Socks with holes in them
- Socks without holes in them
- Actually just socks in general

- Food that wiggles when you try to eat it, i.e. spaghetti/noodles/worms.

HE DOESN'T LIKE BATHS:
- Or showers
- Or rain
- Or water
- Or swimming.

HE DISLIKES:
- The sea (even though he's never seen it)
- Loud noises
- Bright lights

- The dark
- Strange sounds
- Anything that crunches
- Gloves
- Mittens
- Kittens
- Chips
- Chocolate
- Chocolate chips
- Hats
- Cats
- Bats
- Dogs
- Frogs
- Mooses
- Gooses
- Mousses (especially strawberry flavour)
- Meeces (which is what he calls lots of mices. I mean *mice*.)
- Games
- Fun of any kind.

HE ISN'T KEEN ON:
- Singing
- Laughing
- Dancing
- Any form of bottom shaking
- Cake (ESPECIALLY birthday cake)
- Flowers
- Puddles
- Cuddles (well, no one has actually ever cuddled him)
- Anything that sparkles
- Dens
- The colour red.

HE IS ALSO CERTAINLY NOT RAVING ABOUT:
- Warm blankets
- Hot chocolate
- Having a nice sit-down
- Smiling.

And if there was one thing The Grumpus doesn't like more than anything else in the whole world it is this:

CHRIS

And *that* is what this story is about.

CHAPTER 3

IN WHICH SOME GLUM THOUGHTS ARE THOUGHT ABOUT WHILST SCRATCHING

Once upon a winter's morning, The Grumpus stood in the door of his house, scratching his armpit with a fork. He was in a ferociously grumpy mood.

Firstly, his alarm clock had been too loud. The bell had ding-dinged so loudly he'd thought his ears were going to fall off. Then his blankets had been too warm and too itchy, and when he threw them off, he found his bedroom was far too cold.

Then he had, like every morning, woken up on the wrong side of the bed, which had made him grumpier still, mainly because this meant he'd clambered out of bed and walked face first into a wall.

But as he stood there in the doorway, scritch-scratching his armpit and thinking, his mood grew even more ferociously crabby. There was a crisp, crackly coating of frost on the ground, which was too white, twinkly and crunchy as far as The Grumpus was concerned. There was also a chill in the air, a shiver, and just fading from sight as the weak sun rose were the last faint traces of the Northern Lights dancing across the morning sky.

For most people, the sight of all this would have been magical, but not for The Grumpus. His eyebrows crashed together. He knew what it all meant. What it all added up to . . .

'Hmph!' he grunted. He held one of his large hands up to one of his ears and waggled it this way and that. The sound of Jolly Music and Jingling Bells were on the breeze, which could only mean one thing: Christmas was almost here.

He tutted and went inside and slammed the door. Then he slammed it again for good measure.

It was the same every year. Frost. A Chill in the air. Magical Night-Time Lights in the sky.

Then:

Jolly Noises.

Snow.

Merriment.

(He made a mental note to add all of those things to that list of things he Absolutely Does Not Like at All, Thank You Very Much.)

Then, of course, after that was the big day itself, with all the hooting and trumpeting nonsense that that involved.

The Grumpus stomped about a bit with his hands on his hips, and kicked at dustballs on his carpet. (The Grumpus didn't like cleaning.) 'Stupid Christmas!' he huffed. 'Stupid sparkly, twinkly, jingly-jangly, crinkly-wrapped-up-with-a-shiny-bow Christmas!' Everyone was about to go bonkers with excitement about it. He just knew it.

'Well, I'm not going to go bonkers!' grouched The Grumpus to himself, as he scratched his belly. He was going to do what he did every year – grumble and huff around his house, and then he would spend the whole of Christmas Day sitting in the dark with his arms firmly folded, tutting.

He nodded decisively.

Yes. That was an excellent plan. Clever, The Grumpus, he thought.

And he would start right this very second.

But at that very second his tummy suddenly rumbled. *Well*, he thought, *I'll start right after I've had something to eat.*

Now, you might be wondering if there was ANYTHING that The Grumpus actually DID like, and the answer to that is, surprisingly, yes.

He liked precisely three things.

The first of these was Brussels sprouts. Green and stinky, boiled until they were squishy, Brussels sprouts. The Grumpus ate them every day, for every meal, morning, noon and night. And a big bowl of steaming Brussels sprouts was what he was going to have right now for breakfast.

'Just the thing,' he said, as cheerfully as The Grumpus could muster, 'to set me up for a good day of GRUMBLING.' And he galumphed to his Brussels sprout cupboard and threw open the doors.

The cupboard was BARE.

The Grumpus stared at the empty cupboard for a moment, blinked, then closed the doors.

He waited another moment, opened them once more and looked again.

Still not a sprout to be seen anywhere!

He closed his eyes.

He took a deep breath.

Then he went ABSOLUTELY. CRACKERS.

He shouted and grumped and stamped and roared.

He yelled rude words that I'm not allowed to write here (but I can tell you that 'bum' featured prominently) and crashed about for ten minutes. Eventually he flopped, face down, onto the floor.

His belly rumbled again. He told it to pipe down.

No Brussels sprouts in the house was A DISASTER. The Grumpus sighed. He would have to go shopping, and he LOATHED shopping.

And if you think he's in a bad mood already . . . Oh boy. Wait until you find out what happens next . . . !

CHAPTER 4

IN WHICH A SHOPPING EXPEDITION DOES NOT GO COMPLETELY TO PLAN

The Grumpus spent the next few minutes crashing about the house like a thunderstorm, getting ready for his trip to the vegetable shop.

He rammed his feet into his shoes and shouted with annoyance. He didn't like undoing shoelaces and he didn't like doing them up again, so he just shoved and wiggled his feet into his pumps, often falling over in the process. He huffed like a hog, picked himself up and reached for his jumper.

Ah. The jumper. While The Grumpus is snorting and huffing his way into it, I can tell you all about that.

The jumper was the second of the three things that The Grumpus actually liked. It was very old, very grubby and had holes in both the elbows. It was far too small for him, and great acres of arm and tummy poked out of its ends. But what made it special, in The Grumpus's eyes, was that right across his belly it had a row of big knitted sprouts. The Grumpus thought it was the bee's knees and he never went anywhere without it.

Once he had squeezed himself into it, he reached for the third and final thing he actually liked: The Stick. Capital T for The and capital S for Stick.

Now, in many ways The Stick was just a stick.

A large one, yes, but it was just a big, old, branchy bit of stick. For The Grumpus, however, The Stick was his only friend. He didn't like people or any creatures at all, but he could, he felt, be friends with a stick.

The main reason why he liked The Stick was because it didn't answer back. The Grumpus could grump and grouch to it all day long and The Stick wouldn't say anything in return. And, because it was a stick, it didn't have any particular feelings at all about Christmas.

'Christmas! Harrumph!' growled The Grumpus, and he waggled The Stick so it nodded in agreement. Then, with his jumper on and The Stick in hand, The Grumpus slammed out of his house and marched to the sprout shop.

✢   ✢   ✢

The Grumpus's house somehow looked like it was frowning. It sat at the edge of the town, separated by a clump of drooping, sighing trees. He crunched past them that morning on his furious, frosty walk to the shops, remembering this time last year when he had found someone trying to decorate their bare branches with twinkling Christmas lanterns.

Cripes, had he been cross!

He'd hoicked the merry decorator up by the back of their trousers with The Stick, swung them around in the air and hurled them into a bush. Twinkly Christmas lights indeed!

'Silly Christmas!' he glowered.

The closer to town The Grumpus marched, the grumpier he became. He discovered that his suspicions first thing that morning had been correct. The frost had brought with it the first fizzing excitement for Christmas. Great clouds of steam billowed from his ears as all around him townsfolk bustled about, twittering and nattering, giddy with Christmas cheer.

There were songs being sung, lights being hung and enormous piles of presents wrapped in glitzy paper being carried about in teetering towers. Tinsel and baubles and swags of holly were draped from roofs and windowsills. In the centre of town, a gang of very busy people were heaving a glittering fir tree into position.

'Stupid Christmas!' growled The Grumpus as the crowds parted in his path. Everyone slunk away (as always) as the huffing, puffing bundle of grump blundered into Frau Butternut's Vegetable and Fruit Emporium.

A little bell tinkled as the door swung open, and The Grumpus, snorting with fury, plucked the bell from its bracket, stomped on it, stomped on it again for good measure, and then threw it in the bin. All the shoppers stopped and fell silent. Very quickly, they busied themselves with the potatoes and turnips. They muttered in Hushed Tones as The Grumpus stomped through the shop, walloping his head off a ceiling lamp as he did so.

Behind the counter, Frau Butternut stopped polishing a parsnip. 'Oh hello, Mr The Grumpus,' she said nervously. 'And wh-what can I do for you for you this fine festive m-morning?'

'Sprouts,' said The Grumpus. 'Brussels sprouts. All of them.'

Frau Butternut slid her spectacles up her nose and fussed with the collar of her high-necked blouse. 'Sprouts?' she said. 'Sprouts, you say? Are y-you sure? Couldn't I interest you in . . . um . . . in a nice, um . . . cabbage?'

The Grumpus glowered under his bushy eyebrows.

'Or . . . or a gorgeous gourd?' She half-heartedly held up something large and knobbly.

'SPROUTS,' said The Grumpus again, even more grumpily this time. 'ALL OF THEM.'

Frau Butternut gulped and started polishing her parsnip as casually as she could, but the lenses of her spectacles had started to fog up. 'Well, you see the – the thing is, Mr The Grumpus . . .' she twittered. 'The fact is . . . Well, what I'm trying to say – well, tell you really, is . . .'

Everyone in the shop held their breath.

'YES?' said The Grumpus.

'Well . . .' wobbled Frau Butternut. 'There aren't any left. I-I-I just sold the very last one a moment ago . . .'

Steam slowly started to waft out from The Grumpus's ears. 'Who to?' he said.

Frau Butternut polished furiously. 'That mouse

over there . . .' she said, and she pointed behind The Grumpus to where a tiny mouse wearing a fancy hat and carrying a large sprout had been trying to tiptoe out of the shop as quietly as she could manage. The Grumpus spun around on the spot and glared at the mouse. She grinned nervously at him and then darted out of the door as fast as she could.

'N-no more left, I'm afraid,' said Frau Butternut.

The Grumpus closed his eyes. (Oh no!)

The Grumpus took a deep breath. (Oh cripes!)

The Grumpus threw back his head. (Uh-oh! Here we go . . .)

And . . .

CHAPTER 5

IN WHICH THE GRUMPUS
EXPRESSES HIMSELF CLEARLY

'AAAAAAAAAAAAAAARGHHHHH!' said The Grumpus (grumpily).

CHAPTER 6

IN WHICH A DASTARDLY, DREADFUL PLAN IS MADE (OH CRIKEY!)

Now, The Grumpus was ALWAYS grumpy – everyone knew that. But nobody could ever, NEVER remember him being THIS grumpy! He was beyond furious.

His face slowly turned bright, beetroot pink, and steam drifted in a worrying manner from both his ears and his nostrils. He turned on the heels of his shoes and stormed out of the shop, walloping his head on the door frame as he left.

He stood in the main square of the town with his hands on his hips, snorting like a big, sweaty hog.

CHRISTMAS! The problem was ALWAYS Christmas! Christmas was the reason he had no sprouts! Christmas was the time of year when everybody else STOLE the sprouts that were rightfully his. Everywhere he looked, there it was – Christmas! The tree! Christmas!

The decorations! Christmas! The twinkly lights, the jangly music, the jingling bells! Christmas, Christmas, Christmas!

And no sprouts left for him.

His anger ERUPTED like a volcano.

He jumped up and down on the spot, growling like a tiger. Then he stomped about, roaring like a lion. All the townsfolk scarpered and scrambled out of his way. They skedaddled with their piles of sparkly wrapping paper and hid in shops, peering out from behind chestnut toasters and frosty street lamps.

'CHRISTMAS!' The Grumpus grumbled, as he pulled boughs of holly down from around the bandstand. 'CHRISTMAS!' he grouched, as he hurled baubles into a bin. 'STINKING! TWINKLY! JANGLY! JINGLY! SPARKLY! STUPID! CHRISTMAS!' he growled, as with an enormous HEAVE he pushed over the big Christmas tree in the middle of the square. It crashed to the ground with a clinking, clanking crash, scattering decorations all over the place.

'CHRISTMAS should be stopped!' he cried.

And as he said that, a seed of an idea popped into his mind. As he furiously marched about, his anger watered the seed, and the idea started to grow like one of the gourds in Frau Butternut's shop – large and knobbly. Soon it filled nearly all the space in his grumpy, grouchy head.

As he passed Herr Gutentag's Bookshop, something caught his eye. He grinned – but not nicely like you do for your school photograph. Oh no! The Grumpus grinned a grim, very-pleased-with-himself sort of smile that snaked across his face until it almost reached his eyebrows.

When The Grumpus had started his rumpus, all the shoppers leaving Herr Gutentag's had thrown their new purchases to the ground and dashed back into the shop. Once safely inside they had put hardback books on their heads for protection, and peered out of the windows with wild, worried eyes.

As a result, the ground in front of the building was now littered with books. Big books, thin books, books with pictures and boring books with no pictures. There were even some maps on the floor, and one of these, would you believe, was now right by The Grumpus's left foot. It was this that he had noticed.

It fluttered open as a chilly breeze huffed across the frosty square.

The Grumpus picked up the map and looked at it. His eyes narrowed as they darted all across the squiggly lines and splodgy shapes. Roads and lanes and hills and mountains danced in front of The Grumpus as he searched

for what he was looking for and then – AHA! – he found it.

THE NORTH POLE.

The Grumpus prodded the words so roughly that he poked a hole in the paper.

The North Pole. The home of Father Christmas. The headquarters of Christmas.

The Grumpus smiled one of his awful smiles again as the idea in his head sprouted into a fully formed plan.

It was a Dreadful plan!

It was Dastardly plan!

You will cry 'OH NO!' when you find out what it is!

Are you ready?

'I'm going to go to the North Pole,' The Grumpus announced, his voice booming and echoing all around the square, 'and I am going to STOP CHRISTMAS ONCE AND FOR ALL!'

(OH NO!)

CHAPTER 7

IN WHICH THE GRUMPUS SETS OFF AND HAS DREADFUL THOUGHTS AND NOTIONS

The Grumpus didn't even go home to fetch his toothbrush. With the map roughly folded and crinkled up under his jumper, and with The Stick gripped firmly in his hand and his chin jutting out, he set off immediately just as he was.

He stomped across the cobbles and lolloped, livid, down the lanes. He was soon out of the town and furiously marching across frosty fields and empty, wintery meadows.

Despite his crossness, The Grumpus was also feeling rather pleased with himself. A thrill of excitement quivered from his toes to his legs, up under his jumper, until it arrived at his face. It turned his cheeks pink and made him grin that terrible grin again.

'Yes!' he said to The Stick, gleefully. 'How clever I am! I'm going to march up to Father Christmas's front door, knock on it, and then I'll . . . I'll . . .' He floundered a bit and his stomping slowed to a shuffle. 'What am I going to do?' he said. But The Stick didn't reply.

The Grumpus crinkled his brow and thought hard. He knew without doubt that he WOULD succeed in his task, but now that he was on his way, he did think that he needed a bit of a plan for once he actually got to the North Pole.

He picked up his pace again as the cogs in his head started whirring. 'Really . . .' he said to The Stick, 'there are lots of ways I could stop Christmas from happening. I could simply put Father Christmas down

on the ground and then sit on him with my arms folded. He wouldn't be able to move then, so delivering presents would be impossible!'

He looked at The Stick for encouragement, but, of course, none came.

'You're right!' he agreed begrudgingly. 'That plan isn't Dastardly or Dreadful enough . . .'

The Grumpus continued to think.

'Perhaps . . .' he mused, 'Father Christmas will have a big pot of glue in his workshop and I can use that to stick his silly sleigh to the ground.'

Once again The Stick didn't say anything, but The Grumpus decided that this plan was better. 'And if there wasn't any glue, maybe there would be a tin of treacle . . .' he said. 'Treacle is VERY sticky and would work perfectly too. With the sleigh stuck tight, Father Christmas wouldn't be able to fly about delivering any stupid presents to anyone!'

The Grumpus liked the sound of that.

'Or,' he continued, his brain fizzing with plans now, 'I could hide his reindeer! Or . . .'

He looked at The Stick in his hand. 'Or I could use you,' said The Grumpus to his twiggy friend. 'I could throw each present up into the air and then use you like a catapult to fire them all over the place! By the time old Father Beardy-Pants and his helpers have found them all again, it will be too late. It will be morning and Christmas won't have happened. What do you think of that?'

The Stick was silent as always, but The Grumpus knew what it would be thinking if it could think. It would be thinking what he was thinking himself:

'Extremely clever!' bellowed The Grumpus, and for the first time since he'd stormed out of his town, he stopped walking. He put his hands on his hips and rocked back and forth on his heels, smiling and feeling immensely pleased with himself. It was only then that he looked around and he suddenly didn't feel quite so smug.

He realized that he must have been walking for hours, because it appeared to suddenly be night-time, and he was now in a forest. The cold winter sun had slipped away and all around him the great shapes of trees jutted darkly into the cloudless sky. Far in the distance, wafts of beautiful blue-green Northern Lights glimmered and glinted through the stars like magical ribbons.

Now that he'd stopped walking, the cold crept up on The Grumpus and made him shiver. A fresh carpet of thick frost crackled under his feet and his breath became clouds in front of his face.

He realized that he was exhausted and needed to sleep.

'Hmmm . . .' grumbled The Grumpus, a fresh wave of the grumps growling inside him. He wished now that he hadn't been quite so quick to set off. He should, he thought, have gone home to fetch his blanket at least.

He scooped up a handful of crispy dried leaves and spread them out on the forest floor. It really was jolly cold. His bottom shivered as he lay down on them. He closed his eyes.

'Silly Christmas!' grouched The Grumpus sleepily. 'We'll show them all, won't we, Stick?'

He made The Stick nod again and then The Grumpus immediately fell asleep.

Little did he know that he was in for quite a surprise in the morning.

Miles from the frosty forest where
The Grumpus was snoring, far over
fields and a frozen sea, the thing
that was creaking and groaning,
groaned and creaked.

It winced and it wobbled in the wind.

Above it in the star-speckled sky,
the magical ribbons of light
fizzed and flickered.

On. Off. On. Off.

And beneath it, the snow trembled . . .

CHAPTER 8

IN WHICH THE GRUMPUS
IS SURPRISED TO FIND HIMSELF
ENTIRELY SURROUNDED BY . . .

RABBITS!

The Grumpus closed his eyes again – squeezed them shut – and shook his head. Slowly, he opened them and peeked through his icy eyelashes.

Nope! He hadn't been imagining it! He was surrounded, ENTIRELY SURROUNDED, by rabbits. They were all looking at him beadily and blinking in an excitable manner. One was even sitting on his tummy – how dare they! – poised to poke him on the nose with a large carrot, which it hastily hid behind its back.

The Grumpus grunted grumpily. RABBITS! Another thing he would have to go back and add to the list of things he Absolutely Does Not Like at All, Thank You Very Much. It didn't matter that he'd never met one before; he already knew that they weren't his cup of

Brussels sprout-flavoured tea. Silly furballs. And the noise they were making! All squeaking with excitement.

It had been a long, cold night and he was now half frozen, covered in frost and achy all over. He was in no mood for Nonsense, especially not Rabbit Nonsense, which, as everyone knows, is the most nonsensy sort of Nonsense there is.

He flicked the rabbit off his stomach and clambered slowly to his feet. The bunnies fell silent.

The snowy-white rabbit with the large glasses who had been pinged rather rudely from her original place on his stomach dusted herself off and sized The Grumpus up. She didn't seem concerned by his frowning eyebrows or his surly, sulky face.

'Oooooh!' she squeaked excitedly. 'You'll do perfectly! You're just what we need!' Then she turned to the other fluffy-bottomed members of her gang and announced in a voice exactly one hundred times her size, 'LET PROJECT SNOW GLOBE BEGIN!'

The rabbits immediately went bonkers and started to run around in a blur of bobble hats and pompom tails.

'Project what?' said The Grumpus. He was still half asleep and too confused to remember to be completely grumpy.

The lead rabbit – the one with the loud voice and the spectacles – tutted cheerfully and motioned some of the larger rabbits over. Together, they all started to push

The Grumpus through the trees and into a clearing. 'Project Snow Globe!' said the rabbit. 'Today's the day, and you are just what we need – someone tall enough to help us put up all the dangly things! Here – start tying these to those branches.'

Utterly bewildered, The Grumpus looked down and found that the rabbits were loading up his hands with mountains of carefully cut-out paper snowflakes. Steam started to waft out of his ears again and the grumps started to rumble inside him.

Tie paper snowflakes to the trees? NONSENSE! Christmassy, rabbity nonsense! He wouldn't do it! He had his Dastardly, Dreadful Plan to complete and the North Pole was still a long way away.

The Grumpus threw the snowflakes on the floor.

'NO!' he barked.

'SHAN'T!' he growled.

'I HAVE SOMEWHERE TO BE!' he gnarled.

'Where?' asked the rabbit in charge, with her paws on her hips.

The Grumpus opened his mouth to announce his Dastardly, Dreadful Plan, but he stopped himself just in time. *No* . . . he thought, looking to The Stick for support. *I mustn't tell her. If I do, they'll all try to stop me from stopping Christmas . . .*

'Well,' said the rabbit, cheerfully, 'whatever it is, it can't be THAT important, so you definitely have time to

help us with our surprise! There's a good boy!' And she patted him nicely on the ankle.

The Grumpus glowered and was just about to shout, 'I am NOT a good boy – I am The Grumpus,' when one of the other bunnies tapped the rabbit with the spectacles on the arm and pointed across the clearing to a little hill. The Grumpus looked to where she was pointing, and saw that the hill was actually a cave with a tidy front door set into the entrance. A chimney poked out of the top, from which a little silvery sliver of smoke had started to snake.

The rabbit clasped her face in her paws. Her whiskers wobbled in panic. 'QUICK, EVERYONE!' she cried excitedly. 'She's awake and making her tea! Ooooh! She'll be out before you know it – we haven't a moment to lose.'

The rabbits started to run around busily again, and The Grumpus found his arms refilled with even more paper snowflakes. 'Please can you tie them to all the branches you can reach?' cried the rabbit with the spectacles. 'And I'll explain everything. QUICK! QUICK!'

And, despite himself, and for the first time ever, The Grumpus actually did something somebody asked him to do. And as he did so (with grinding teeth), he wondered what was going on.

CHAPTER 9

IN WHICH THE GRUMPUS FINDS HIS PLAN DISRUPTED FOR THE FIRST TIME AS HE GETS INVOLVED WITH ANOTHER ONE

For the next twenty minutes or so, The Grumpus found himself in the centre of a blizzard of activity. Bunnies dashed about around him, hopping and tumbling from underground burrows and doors set into the thick trunks of trees, bringing with them white blankets and white quilts and fluffy white towels.

The rabbit with the spectacles stood on a tree stump and directed her chums to start spreading their belongings out on the ground. Meanwhile, more and more carefully cut-out paper snowflakes were handed to The Grumpus, and when the rabbit asked him to carry on tying them to all the branches, he was too dazed and confused to argue.

As he did so, the bunny with the spectacles explained what was happening.

'Do you know Grandma Bear?' she asked.

The Grumpus shook his head. He'd never met a bear before, but he decided on the spot to add them to his I-Do-Not-Like List. He also decided to add grandmas to that list (even though he'd never met one of those before either).

'Where on earth have you been?' said the rabbit. 'EVERYONE knows Grandma Bear. She lives in that cave over there – the one with the chimney – and ooooh, we absolutely LOVE Grandma Bear. She isn't REALLY our grandma of course, but we all call her that.'

She stopped to take a breath and to direct a bundle of bunnies who were carrying a large picnic hamper across the clearing. She pointed the way with her carrot, then she used it to prod The Grumpus on the bottom because he had stopped dangling snowflakes for a moment. He swatted at her indignantly with The Stick. Being poked with vegetables was another thing that he did NOT like. He felt his grumpiness building inside him again, and his face threatened to turn red at any moment.

'Well, the thing about Grandma Bear,' she said, 'is that at the First Frost she gets very tired. She pops on her nightie and then that's her asleep until she gets a whiff of the first daffodils in spring. She sleeps for the WHOLE winter. Can you believe that?'

The Grumpus shook his head grouchily again, still bewildered by this nattering bunny and the fact that he was oddly doing as he'd been told.

The rabbit carried on. 'The other night, when we were all meant to be asleep, I had a dreadful thought! I realized that because she always slept through the winter, Grandma Bear has never seen snow! IMAGINE THAT!'

She paused long enough to clasp her paws to her face in horror.

The Grumpus snorted. 'So what?' he said, grumpily. 'Snow is stupid!' He thought Grandma Bear was extremely clever to sleep through it all. He wished he'd had that clever idea.

He looked at the rabbit, hoping she'd be shocked by his grouchiness, but she just laughed and patted his ankle again.

'What a funny thing to say!' She chuckled. 'Snow is WONDERFUL, which is why I've decided to bring winter to Grandma Bear. Look!' she said, and, using the carrot as a pointer again, she waggled it in the direction of the clearing. The Grumpus looked.

It really was quite extraordinary.

Blankets, quilts, towels, jumpers, dishcloths – anything white that the rabbits could get their paws on – had been spread on the ground. And, thanks to The Grumpus's own handiwork, from every spindly winter branch hung a snowflake, each of them dancing in the chilly breeze.

'Why would you do all of this?' grunted The

Grumpus. He couldn't understand why anyone would go to such trouble.

The rabbit giggled.

'Oh you ARE a silly, er . . . well – whatever you are, you are a silly one! We are doing it because Grandma Bear is so kind. She looks after us and gives us hugs and makes us carrot porridge and untangles our ears and fluffs our tails and . . . and well – ooooh! – she's just LOVELY. And we wanted to say thank you to her before she has her snooze! And Christmas is the best time of the year, isn't it? It's such a shame she misses it . . .'

The Grumpus was even more confused. Say thank you? HUMPH! He'd never done that in his entire life. Silly bunnies! He decided he'd had quite enough of their nonsense. He smoothed down his eyebrows, picked up The Stick and started to march off through the forest. He urgently needed to get on with his Dastardly, Dreadful Plan.

With any luck he'd not have lost too much time and would be at the North Pole before bedtime.

Well, maybe . . .

He should check the map.

He was just about to take it out from under his jumper when his hand was grabbed by the rabbit.

Yuck! The Grumpus didn't like hand-holding at all!

'Where are you going, Mr Silly?' she cried. 'You

can't go now. Look, Grandma Bear is here!'

And she was.

From the entrance of the cave house ambled a very big, very old bear, wearing a thick cardigan, with a steaming mug of tea in her paw. She looked very sleepy, but her eyes grew wide with astonishment as she looked about and saw what the rabbits (and The Grumpus) had been up to.

'Goodness!' she said. 'What's all this?'

All at once and all together, the rabbits chittered and chattered and gabbled and gibbled as they told Grandma Bear their plan. The more she heard, the more Grandma Bear's ears waggled and her nose went pink.

'And . . .' said Spectacles Bunny, when most of the giddiness had died down, 'our new friend helped too.'

The Grumpus looked around to see who she was talking about. He couldn't see anyone. He turned back and was surprised to see all the bunnies and Grandma Bear looking at HIM.

Me? A new friend? he thought. *HUMPH . . . I'm not their bloomin' friend.*

Suddenly, he squirmed a bit. A funny feeling had started under his jumper. It was a tickling feeling. Not an itch, but maybe a tingle. The Grumpus scratched at himself, then tried very slowly to sidestep his way out of the clearing. But he couldn't. He was, once again, completely surrounded.

'He says he's got somewhere to go and something IMPORTANT to do . . .' continued the rabbit with the spectacles. 'But he must stay, mustn't he?'

'Oh absolutely!' said Grandma Bear, and all the bunnies nodded. Some of them standing close to The Grumpus even hugged him around his ankles.

The Grumpus sighed. There was no escape. He'd have to stay until he could work out how to scarper and get on with his Dastardly, Dreadful Plan. It was very important that he kept on schedule so Christmas could be stopped.

He shook the bunnies away from his ankles and folded his arms crossly. *Friend* . . . he thought, and snorted. That was another word for his list of dislikes. Who needs friends when you can be a grumpy grouch?

But try as he might to ignore it, he couldn't escape the funny feeling tingling under his special jumper. And beneath his grumpy, frowning eyebrows, he realized his cheeks had turned as rosy and as pink as Grandma Bear's nose.

CHAPTER 10

In Which The Grumpus Finds Himself Joining In

At first The Grumpus stood awkwardly and crossly at the edge of the clearing, gripping hold of The Stick and trying, whenever he could, to sidestep sneakily away from the group. But before long he couldn't help his ears twisting this way and that to listen as the bunnies explained their plan to Grandma Bear. Curiosity tugged at him, and he crept closer to hear more clearly.

Winter, the rabbits seemed to think, was full of Exciting Opportunities. There were lots of things you could do with your friends to make the most of the magical season.

'Hmph!' snorted The Grumpus. He whispered to The Stick, 'You'd need friends first, and I don't have any of them (apart from you), thank goodness!' But he continued to listen.

The rabbits were saying that snow made everything special. It blanketed the earth and made it sparkle like it had been brushed with magic dust.

The Grumpus was surprised by that. He'd always thought snow was AWFUL. It was just cold and soggy, two things he loathed. But as he looked around the clearing, at the transformation he and the rabbits had made, he had to admit that it did look like it had been sprinkled with magic. And, of course, this was only pretend snow.

The real thing, thought The Grumpus, looking at it with fresh eyes under his surly, knitted-together brows, would probably be even better.

He cleared his throat, shocked to find himself thinking such a non-grumpy thought. He frowned harder to make up for it.

The rabbit in charge – the one with the glasses – had a long list of exciting things to do to make sure Grandma Bear got a full snowy-day experience. As the bunnies got ready, The Grumpus stood nervously behind a tree, watching. But it wasn't long before he felt something tugging at his hand. He looked down to find several rabbits.

'NO! NO! NO!' he protested, but they didn't seem to hear him, despite the fact they had very long ears. They heaved and pulled him into the action.

'But I don't know what to do!' he grouched at them.

'That's OK!' they chirped all together. 'We'll help you!'

And they did. They all explained to him what was going on, and in a wiggle of a fluffy tail, The Grumpus found himself sliding down the side of a blanket-covered hill on a tea tray. Over and over he whizzed with Grandma Bear, whooping as she and the bunnies held on tightly to him.

The wind whipping through his hair felt exciting.

Then they all busily made a snowman – well, really it was a snow bear – using piles of fluffy pillows. The Grumpus once again found himself very useful because he was just the tall creature they needed who could pop a beetroot on the snow bear in place of a nose. (The rabbit with the glasses did have to tell The Grumpus to make the snow bear look a bit less grumpy . . .)

Then it was time for a snowball fight.

On one side of the clearing stood Grandma Bear with half of the bunnies, and on the other side of the clearing was The Grumpus with his team of rabbits.

As soon as the rabbit with the spectacles cried 'GO!' the air was filled with balled-up sock snowballs, as both teams tried to plonk each other on the head with them. The whole clearing was filled with whoops and hollers and excited squeaks of delight.

The Grumpus looked on, feeling unsure. He didn't know how to play games. He'd never had anyone to play

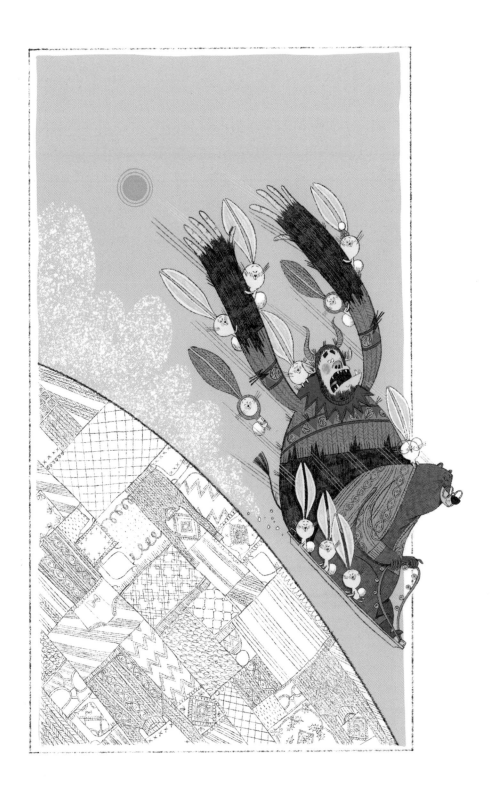

with – The Stick couldn't play games, after all. Therefore, The Grumpus had decided that all games were Stupid and that he didn't like them At All.

He looked from under his eyebrows at the rabbits. They all seemed to be so jolly and giddy with excitement, and he realized that he had never felt like they did now. 'Silly games,' he hissed to The Stick. 'Silly rabbits too!'

But as he watched the fun, he felt something bubble inside him.

Was it a big burp? he wondered. But no! Whatever it was, it made him reach down and pick up a ball of socks and hurl it across the clearing. He was joining in!

But UH-OH! The pair of socks The Grumpus had thrown gave a cry of surprise as it flew through the air. It wasn't a pair of socks at all. It was a fluffy white tail, and it had a rabbit attached. In his excitement, The Grumpus had accidentally picked up one of the rabbits instead of a pair of socks!

The bunny landed with a *twang* in some of the dangling snowflakes. The Grumpus lolloped over to untangle her. He felt hot around the neck of his jumper, but to his surprise the bunny in the tree just giggled. She didn't seem to mind a bit that she'd been mistaken for a snowball!

As he reached up to untangle her, the map hidden under his jumper poked out. The rabbit with the spectacles, who was standing beside The Grumpus, supervising him, couldn't help but notice it.

She saw green shapes for the forests and fields, and she spotted the hole poked through the great expanse of white with the words 'THE NORTH POLE' written on the crumpled-up paper beside it. She thought this was very interesting.

With the other bunny set down neatly on the ground again, Grandma Bear decided that it was time for them all to have a nice sit-down and something warm to drink. The sun had started to slip down low behind the bare trees, and fresh frost was glittering and crackling in the air.

The picnic basket was pulled out and everyone sat around it, nibbling Christmas cookies and drinking mugs of hot chocolate.

The Grumpus sniffed at his mug suspiciously before working up the courage to try some of the frothy drink. He looked at The Stick for reassurance, but The Stick said nothing.

The Grumpus took a sip. Hmmm . . . not bad, but it would probably taste even better if it had some Brussels sprouts stirred into it, he thought.

As the sky grew darker, Grandma Bear's eyelids started to droop. She yawned one yawn after another. She looked very sleepy indeed. 'What a nice day I've had,' she said with a lovely, dreamy smile. 'I have always wondered what I was missing while I was snoozing, and now I know.

I'll dream of you all having fun in the real snow all winter long.'

She looked around and her nose turned very pink.

'How lucky I am to have such lovely friends,' she said, and she hugged all of the rabbits.

The Grumpus watched.

Fun . . .

The Grumpus hadn't had fun before and he certainly hadn't today. Well, actually, he thought, maybe, just maybe the afternoon had been . . . yes, maybe just a little, teeny, tiny bit fun.

And friends?

That was another thing he'd never had. He'd always been on his own because – well, he'd never really had any other choice. Whether it was his size or his grumpy face or his large, stomping feet, he wasn't sure, but people had always scarpered whenever he was near. So, in return, he had just avoided them as best he could. It had always just been him and The Stick, and that was just the way he liked it . . .

Once again, that strange feeling prickled under his jumper. He scratched it but it didn't go away.

Before he could think on it any further, The Grumpus found himself being hugged tightly by Grandma Bear. The Grumpus stood awkwardly as she squeezed him. He didn't like hugs because he'd never been hugged before.

'I hope you have a good journey, wherever you are going,' she said to him. She waved to them all sleepily, before plodding off to her cave. Within a few minutes, deep snores came rumbling out of the chimney.

Journey! thought The Grumpus suddenly, and inside him storm clouds whipped up as the grumps started to billow in.

Stupid rabbits! he thought.

Stupid Grumpus! he thought.

My Dastardly, Dreadful Plan! I'm late now! he thought.

He had many miles to cover to get to the North Pole and STOP CHRISTMAS, and he'd let himself get distracted by fluffy-bottomed nonsense.

As the rabbits busily tidied up their things, The Grumpus snatched up The Stick, and without even saying goodbye, he stomped off through the darkening forest.

His mind whirred as it ticked over the day and the journey ahead. He was so lost in his thoughts as he trudged through the woods that he didn't notice real snowflakes starting to fall softly around him.

And he also didn't notice that he was being followed . . .

CHAPTER 11

IN WHICH THE GRUMPUS FINDS EVERYTHING GOES DOWNHILL RAPIDLY

The Grumpus crashed along, snorting like an angry hog. A truly frightful mood had descended on him once more, and he didn't notice the snow around him until it was at least ankle height.

'HMPH!' he harrumphed.

All that messing about with those silly rabbits meant he would now have to march ALL night if he had any hope of reaching the North Pole in time to STOP CHRISTMAS.

Just think, he thought, *how far I would have travelled if I hadn't been interrupted by those furballs.*

He was just working himself up to have a really terrific grump when one of his ears swivelled around to face behind him.

What had it heard?

The Grumpus listened.

A crack: the sound of a twig snapping in two.

The Grumpus glared into the darkness. The snow on the ground (real snow, not blankets and towels this time) created an eerie glow through the skeleton trees.

'HELLO?' grumbled The Grumpus, and he heard his voice leap back at him as it bounced from tree to tree to tree.

'HELLO!

Hello!

'ello!

lo!

oh!'

He waited a moment, but there was no answer. Shaking his head crossly, he turned back and began marching along the bramble path again.

As he walked, he felt all the fur on the back of his neck stand bolt upright and the skin on his ankles prickle with goosebumps. He tried his hardest to concentrate on his grumpy mood, but he couldn't escape the feeling that he was being watched by someone (or something) in the darkness behind him.

He tugged at the hem of his jumper, hoping to pull it low enough to warm his bottom, which was beginning to feel the chill of the cold night air. Urgh! How he loathed having a chilly bottom.

He took a deep breath and shook his head. 'I'm imagining things!' he said to The Stick. 'It's those rabbits! And that bear! And all that "fun" nonsense!' (He said the word 'fun' in the same way you would say something awful like 'sweaty socks' or 'bum'.)

As he continued, that tingly feeling under his jumper started again. *What is that?* he wondered. *I hope I'm not getting poorly. That would REALLY interrupt my Dastardly, Dreadful Plan . . .*

He grinned his dreadful grin as he imagined slapping spoonfuls of treacle to the ground and sticking Father Christmas's sleigh to it. Surely there couldn't be much more forest left? How long could it take to get to the North Pole?

He stopped and reached under his jumper for the map, then he hurried out from the thick clump of trees so he could see it more clearly. Away from their knotted branches, the bright moonlight shone and The Grumpus's heart sank. He looked around and saw that he was standing on a sort of rocky ledge that jutted out over a hillside. Below the ledge were tangly brambles and trees, then, when they thinned out, there were acres of patchwork fields and bumpy hills and mountains.

He consulted the map, running his thick, frozen fingers across the wrinkled paper. He sighed heavily. There was no doubt about it – he had miles and miles still to travel, and, to be honest, he had no real idea where he currently was.

Bloomin' Marvellous!

Steam began wafting from his ears again. The volcano of grumpiness trembled inside and his cheeks grew hot and pink.

He –

SNAP!

He stopped mid-thought and listened.

SNAP!

The Grumpus spun around.

He'd definitely heard something this time.

He held his breath and strained his ears.

Behind the noise of the wind blowing through the trees there was another sound.

Footsteps.

It sounded like footsteps crunching through the snow.

'It's nothing,' The Grumpus told The Stick, who was wedged under his armpit. 'Just normal night noises in the forest. Nothing to be frightened of . . .'

His hands holding the map started to quiver.

The footsteps grew louder and louder.

The Grumpus lifted the map to his face and tried his best to concentrate on the lines and shapes on the paper. If he could just work out where he was, he could scarper onward away from danger.

The footsteps stopped, and now The Grumpus heard heavy breathing. He knew it wasn't his breathing because he was holding his breath.

'Who's there?' he hissed eventually.

There was no answer. He dared himself to peek through the hole in the map he'd made earlier. The hole right beside the words 'THE NORTH POLE'.

He looked.

There was no one there, but he could see footprints. His eyes followed them, his heart thumping in his chest as he realized they led to his feet. They danced in and out of his own deep trail of footprints.

He continued to peer at them, when all of a sudden a face sprang into view. It filled the entire hole he was looking through.

'HELLO!' it said.

The Grumpus nearly leaped out of his skin. He yelped with surprise.

Then two awful things happened almost at the same time.

Firstly, The Grumpus dropped the map and it was instantly snatched away from him by the freezing wind. It was ripped by the nearby brambles and the pieces scattered into the night. (Oh no!)

And then, worse still, The Grumpus staggered backwards.

He stumbled.

He wibbled.

He wobbled.

He teetered on the edge, and then, losing balance (GASP!), he fell off the ledge into the emptiness below...

Creak! Groan!

Groan and Creak!

Suddenly a crack that splits and crackles.

The sky above fizzes and the lights
in the sky falter again.

A group of small faces look on.

They scratch their heads.

Some scratch their beards.

They are very worried indeed.

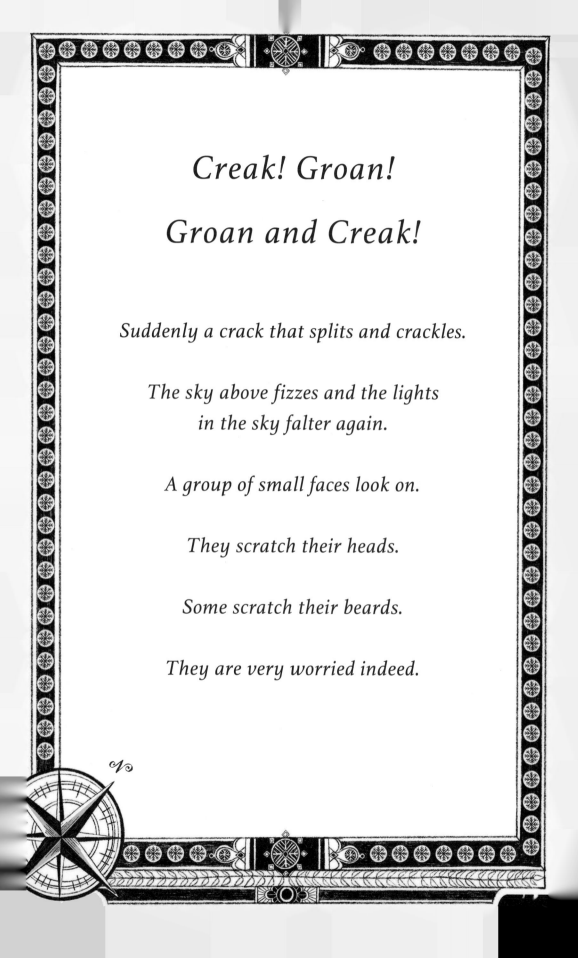

CHAPTER 12

IN WHICH THERE IS A DISASTER AND THE GRUMPUS FINDS HIS PLAN INTERRUPTED FOR THE SECOND TIME

The cold night air whistled past The Grumpus's ears as he tumbled into the darkness. His feet flew up past his head as his arms windmilled, frantically trying to find (without luck) something – anything! – to catch on to.

The Grumpus squeezed his eyes shut and prepared himself for the terrific wallop of his bottom hitting the ground.

But instead of a BUMP! or a CRASH! there was a . . .

BOING!

Huh?

The Grumpus slowly peeled one eye open and looked around him. He was utterly bewildered.

Beneath him were the frozen trees and the cold

ground of the forest, but he was twirling around in the sky above them. He was floating in mid-air! How was this possible? What strange winter magic was this?

He looked up, and everything became clear.

The Grumpus yowled loudly.

'AAAAAAAARRRRRRRRGH!'

His beloved jumper had got caught on a twig on the ledge, and as he had fallen it had unravelled and was now the only thing breaking his fall! He looked at the wiggly, crinkly strand of wool that used to be his jumper and roared again.

'AAAAAAAAAAAAAAARGH!'

Ruined! The whole thing was ruined! He glared indignantly at The Stick (which was still miraculously in his hand and unharmed) to make sure it could see what he was shouting about.

Just then, a face appeared over the rocky ledge above him. It was the same face that had appeared through the hole in the map and had caused The Grumpus to tumble into the night.

'Oh dear! Oh dear! Are you OK down there, Mr Trip-Up?' it said, cheerfully.

The Grumpus looked through his tightly knitted-together eyebrows. Great clouds of angry steam were puffing from his ears like steam from a train engine.

'YOU!' he growled. 'WHAT ARE YOU DOING HERE?'

'I followed you!' said the face above. 'I bet you are

VERY glad I did because now I can help you!'

The face, it turned out, belonged to a rabbit. The one with the glasses. She was now lying down on her belly, face in her paws, peering down at The Grumpus with her legs kicking up happily behind her.

'GLAD?' grumped The Grumpus. 'I wouldn't be . . . be DANGLING here if it hadn't been for you! Why are you here?'

'Well, how was I to know you were going to jump off this hill, you silly turnip!' said the rabbit, giggling. 'Anyway, I followed you because – and you are going to be SO excited when I tell you this – I am coming to the North Pole with you! Isn't that fun? I saw your map poking out of your jumper and I thought, *If he is going to see Father Christmas, I am going with him!* Oh I love Christmas, and you must do too if you are going all that way in this weather. I can't believe that we are really going to see Father Christmas himself. What an adventure we'll have!'

All of this was said at the speed of light, and at the end the rabbit clasped her paws to her excited pink cheeks and squealed with excitement.

But her joy was interrupted by a ripping sound from below, as the already frayed strand of yarn from the unravelled jumper started to uncoil further. The Grumpus dropped another few feet.

'Oh my goodness!' squeaked the rabbit, jumping to

her feet. 'Where are my manners? Here, let me help you!'

'NO!' shouted The Grumpus, his heart pounding with panic in his now exposed chest. It was a long drop down. He just needed time to think. What he didn't need was help. 'You've caused enough trouble! GO AWAY!' he growled.

'Now, there's no need to be like THAT, Mr Grumpy-Chops!' said the rabbit as she carefully unpicked the wool from the tree it was hanging on to and wrapped it around her paw. She heeeeeeeeaaved with all her might, but her efforts made him rise only a few inches. She was very tiny and The Grumpus was very big. There was no way that the little rabbit could haul him to safety on her own.

'DON'T WORRY!' yelled the rabbit from above his head. 'I will go and get help! I'll be back in a minute!'

The Grumpus started to yell 'NO!' but the rabbit had already let go of the yarn and scampered off through the snow. The wool slithered across the frozen ground before zipping off over the side of the hill.

There was a moment when The Grumpus was suspended, frozen in time, before – WHOOSH! – he hurtled though the air and – BUMP! CRASH! CRUNCH! WALLOP! – he landed in the tangled, frozen branches of a tree below.

'Oopsie!' he heard the rabbit cry from somewhere in the distance. 'Sorry!'

CHAPTER 13

IN WHICH AT ONE MOMENT IN THIS CHAPTER THERE IS QUITE A CONFUSION OF SHEEP

'*orry?*' growled The Grumpus to The Stick. 'Sorry? Yes! They will be sorry! If it wasn't for STUPID Christmas, I wouldn't be in this mess!'

And what a mess he was in!

He wasn't sure how long he had been sprawled there, tangled in the branches, but he knew it had been quite a while. Long enough at least for him to work himself up into a tremendous temper. He was well and truly knotted in the twigs, and try as he might to free himself, it was simply impossible.

He lay there, ears steaming, face as red as Father Christmas's suit, grumping to The Stick about everything. Nuisance rabbits. Stinking Christmas. His poor, ruined jumper . . .

He looked down at his belly, at the scribble of unravelled wool sitting on top of it where his jumper used to be. His eyes started to prickle. It was his Most Best belonging, and it was completely and utterly wrecked. He blinked furiously and snorted. If he had been determined to stop Christmas with his Dastardly, Dreadful Plan before, he was doubly determined now. He wouldn't be satisfied until Father Christmas's sleigh was firmly glued to the ground and all the Christmas presents in the North Pole had been scattered as far as the eye could see. In the mood he was in now, he would probably even lock Father Christmas away in a cupboard!

His dastardly thoughts were broken suddenly by the sound of feet and voices below him.

'There he is, the big clumsy carrot!' said the unmistakeably cheery voice of the rabbit.

Then another voice, a new one, said, 'Oh, hello up there!' Then, to the rabbit: 'No problem. We'll have him down in a jiffy.'

The Grumpus looked through the branches. He wasn't sure what he had expected to see, but the sight under him wasn't one he ever would have imagined. Far below, at the base of the tree in which he was stuck, a flock of sheep were all clambering on top of each other to form a tall, wobbly, woolly tower. When they were almost level with The Grumpus, a woman clad in many, many layers of knitted clothing climbed nimbly up them.

While this was happening, the rabbit kept up a steady flow of nattering.

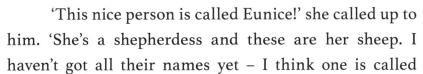

'This nice person is called Eunice!' she called up to him. 'She's a shepherdess and these are her sheep. I haven't got all their names yet – I think one is called Barbara – but they are EVER so nice. You'll love them! Anyway, they were all heading home when I bumped into them. I told them about our exciting adventure and they've come to help rescue you after your little whoops-a-daisy!'

You could have fried an egg on The Grumpus's cheeks, they were so hot with grumpiness.

Eventually the woolly woman reached The Grumpus and smiled at him.

'Hello! Oh, what a tangle,' she said.

The Grumpus grunted but didn't stop her from gently unknotting him and The Stick from the confusion of branches and yarn tying him to the tree. She had fantastically speedy hands, and in no time at all the job was done. The shepherdess threw The Grumpus over her shoulder, clambered down the sheep tower and placed him safely on the ground. She was very strong.

'There,' said Eunice. 'All sorted.'

The Grumpus grunted again. He felt embarrassed and awkward and angry and sad. He wanted to get away from this woman covered in knitwear, and the rabbit and all the sheep, and be grumpy and sad about his jumper on his own. That was where he felt safest. All by himself.

The Grumpus picked up the bundle of wrinkly wool and The Stick and started to stomp off. But he couldn't move. It was only now he was back on firm ground that he realized how cold he was. Every bit of him shivered and shook, and he felt dizzy.

'I think he's going to fall over!' squeaked the rabbit from somewhere near his feet, and the words were hardly out of her mouth when – OH DEAR! – The Grumpus crinkled at the knees and started to tumble to the forest floor.

Everything was spinning, but The Grumpus vaguely realized that at the last minute the shepherdess had caught him. She was carefully carrying him to a neat little sleigh that was sitting nearby. Once safely inside, and with a woollen rug thrown over him, the foggy feeling in his head started to lift. His toes began to thaw out under the blanket.

He heard voices behind him but couldn't make out what they were saying, as there was quite a confusion of sheep around him, all interested to see what was going on.

Eventually he heard the rabbit's squeaky little voice, nattering away as always. 'Oh thank you!' she twittered excitedly. 'I'll go and check he's OK . . .'

As the sleigh slid off through the snow, there was a soft flump beside The Grumpus. The rabbit had landed next to him and nestled herself under the covers by his belly.

'Where are we going?' he rumbled, his head still a bit shivery and confused.

The rabbit patted him gently on the hand. 'Our new friend Eunice is taking us to her house so you can get all warmed up and have a hot drink. Someone who is called Pearl who lives there too is going to sort everything out. Isn't that LOVELY?' She burrowed down beside The Grumpus and closed her eyes. He begrudgingly had to admit to himself that it was good to have her there; she was a little ball of warmth.

'Why would they do that for me?' he asked.

The rabbit yawned and tutted sleepily. 'Because people are kind, silly,' she said. 'Especially at, um –' she gave an even bigger yawn – 'um . . . Christmas.'

And she promptly fell asleep.

As the sleigh skated through the trees and out over the vast snow-covered plains, The Grumpus lay under the blanket, thinking.

'People are kind?' he whispered to The Stick. 'What a silly thing to think!'

In his experience people were strange and frightened, and that in turn made them a bit frightening. Yet here he was, safely rescued from Certain Doom and on his way to somewhere warm with a person and a bunny he had only just met, who both wanted to help simply because they could.

Is this kindness? he wondered. And as he thought that, he suddenly felt dizzy again. That strange feeling from earlier – the fuzzy prickling under his jumper – had come back. Except . . . except his jumper didn't exist any more! It was a ball of wrinkled wool on his lap.

So what was this odd sensation? What was causing it?

✣   ✣   ✣

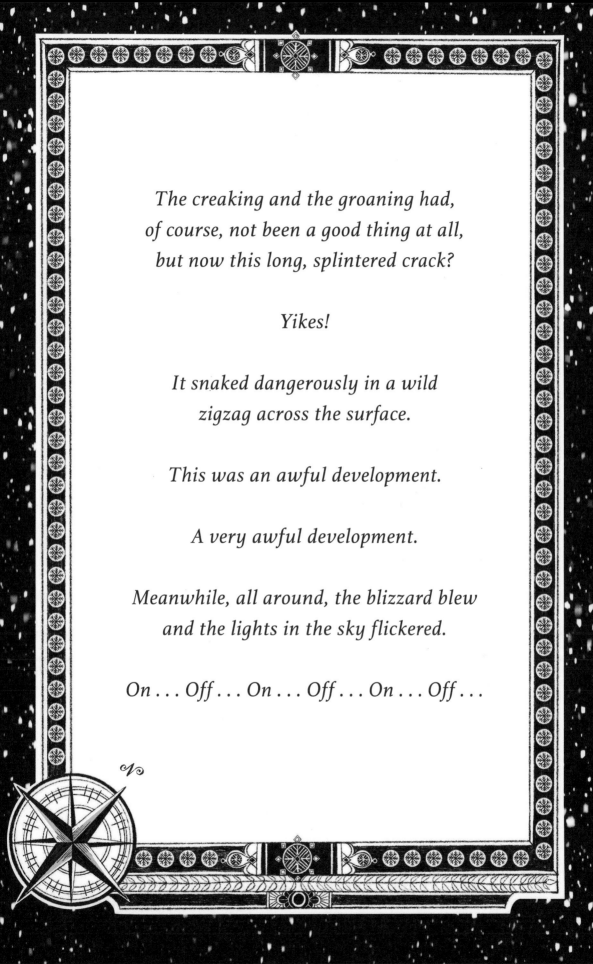

The creaking and the groaning had,
of course, not been a good thing at all,
but now this long, splintered crack?

Yikes!

It snaked dangerously in a wild
zigzag across the surface.

This was an awful development.

A very awful development.

Meanwhile, all around, the blizzard blew
and the lights in the sky flickered.

On . . . Off . . . On . . . Off . . . On . . . Off . . .

CHAPTER 14

IN WHICH THE GRUMPUS
FINDS HIMSELF
DECKING THE HALLS

Eunice and Pearl lived in a small cottage, which, as it was covered in a thick layer of snow, had the look of a sheep about it.

Inside, lamps were lit and a roaring fire crackled in the inglenook. There was a spot of confusion as the sheep were settled into their beds upstairs, but once they were in their pyjamas and snoring their woolly snores, everything was calm and proper introductions could take place.

The rabbit took charge as The Grumpus stood in the dim corner of the room, anxiously tangling and untangling the remains of his jumper in his hands.

'Thank you SO much for letting us come to your house,' the rabbit nattered at full speed. 'It's VERY kind of you to have us here to warm up and things, isn't it?' She nudged The Grumpus, but he didn't say

anything; he just snorted crossly.

The rabbit turned back to Pearl, who was tidying her knitting needles away neatly. 'Don't mind him. He's feeling a bit wobbly because he had his whoopsie over the side of the cliff. It could have been a DISASTER, but then we saved him. Well, Eunice saved him actually. And your nice sheep of course. I helped by being Encouraging. Did you make all of these?' She pointed around the room at all the cosy cushions, rugs and blankets knitted in beautiful and complicated cables and patterns.

Pearl nodded.

The rabbit's eyes boggled. 'You are very clever! OH! Where are my manners? We know YOUR names, but you don't know ours. I am called 586759.' And she shook Pearl and Eunice's hands.

'Goodness!' said Pearl. 'That's quite an unusual name.'

The rabbit sighed. 'Yes, it's not a very good name at all really, is it? It's because I have so many brothers and sisters, my mammy and dada ran out of names after a while and so . . .' She threw up her paws. 'So there you have it: numbers.'

'Well, we need to give you a proper sort of name,' said Eunice. 'I spend all day, every day, counting sheep, so I can't remember any more numbers at all. It needs to be something bunnyish like . . .'

Everyone thought for a moment.

Then, quite to everyone's surprise – including his own – The Grumpus piped up quietly from his corner.

'Furball.'

The rabbit considered this for a moment, then her spectacles started to steam up with joy. 'It's perfect – I love it!' she cried. 'FURBALL! My very own proper name!' And she threw herself on to a pile of cushions and gleefully waggled her legs.

'And what's your name?' said Pearl kindly, turning to the dark shape in the corner.

The Grumpus shifted uncomfortably. 'The Grumpus,' he mumbled.

Furball hopped over and patted The Grumpus on his ankle. 'He's grumpy because his jumper isn't very jumpery any more. It got all untangled when he was dangling from that tree.'

'It had Brussels sprouts on it,' said The Grumpus quietly, his eyes prickling.

'Oh dear, oh dear!' said Pearl. 'Can I see?' And she reached out and gently took the yarn from him. He didn't want to give it to her (*She'll probably RUIN it even more*, he thought) but she took it so nicely, like it was precious, that he let it go.

Pearl ran it through her fingers and looked at it expertly through her glasses. 'Yes,' she said after a moment, 'this certainly has seen better days.'

The Grumpus could feel his cheeks start to burn

with annoyance and crossness. Just as he'd expected. It was ruined. Entirely RUINED. But before he could roar or stomp his feet, Pearl placed the knotted-up wool-that-used-to-be-a-jumper on to her knitting bag and said, mainly to herself, 'Hmm . . . I wonder . . .' Then she looked up and smiled at her guests.

'Listen,' she said to them. 'I think two things are absolutely certain. Firstly, you both must stay the night. It's far too cold outside. And secondly, you must have something to eat!'

Eunice nodded in agreement. Furball was overjoyed with this news and rubbed her belly with anticipation. The Grumpus was less thrilled. He just stood awkwardly again, quietly fuming. He'd never stopped at someone else's house before, and he had a feeling he didn't like it already.

'Now,' said Pearl, 'while we get you some food, I wonder if you both might help me?'

The Grumpus huffed. *What NOW?* he thought. His Dastardly, Dreadful Plan to get to the North Pole and STOP CHRISTMAS was being derailed again. *I could run away*, he considered. He sighed. No, that wouldn't work – he loathed running.

'I wonder if you might help us decorate the cottage? I was just about to do it when you arrived. You make a start while I help Eunice in the kitchen. And I just want to talk to her about a little idea I've had . . .' She

pointed to a pile of overflowing boxes on the table, and the bare little tree standing in the window, before bustling out of the room, stopping only to look at The Grumpus. She squinted at him through her specs, studying him very carefully.

The Grumpus squirmed.

'I bet she doesn't like me at all!' he grumbled to The Stick quietly. *Nobody ever likes me*, he thought, but before he could really get himself angry about that, Furball grabbed his hand and heaved him joyfully over to the box of decorations.

And this was how The Grumpus found himself, ten minutes later, covered in tinsel and holding Furball up so she could place glittering baubles just so on the branches of the Christmas tree. She was beside herself with excitement, but when The Grumpus told her he had never decorated a Christmas tree, she was horrified.

The Grumpus felt awkward again. He couldn't tell her that he usually spent the big day all alone, tutting. Her ears would probably fall off if he did.

'Getting ready for Christmas is SO important,' she said. 'All that fizzy excitement and giddiness in the air! I wait for it all year long. The minute it starts to get chilly we start getting ready at Fluffbottom Burrow – that's what my house is called. We get the tree and we all help to decorate it, and then all my brothers and sisters and I each hang a little light on its branches – so you can imagine how many lights there are! Then we add a few more for those who can't be there or who are a long way away.'

'Why?' grunted The Grumpus. All this Christmas talk was making him cross again. It was everything he disliked. Glittery nonsense! Lights on a silly tree? PAH!

'Oh, The Grumpus!' Furball sighed, handing him a little lantern to hang up. 'It's VERY important because it's about us all being together, even if we aren't. Every time you look at all the little twinkly lights, you think about all your friends and relations, and it makes you feel snug in your belly and around your ears!'

The Grumpus grunted. 'My tree would only have one light for me on it,' he said, half to himself.

Furball laughed. 'Sometimes you are such a silly turnip! It would have AT LEAST two lights – one for me and one for you. See, this one can be my lantern. And this –' she handed him another one – 'can be yours!'

As he looked at it glowing with the others against the darkness outside the window, for some strange reason The Grumpus found his cheeks growing pink.

They stepped back to admire their handiwork. The Grumpus had to admit that the tree looked . . . what was the word?

Pretty!

He pulled a face. He'd NEVER used the word 'pretty' before. Ever. But there was no other way to describe it. In fact, as he looked around, he realized that the whole room looked pretty. It was so cosy and warm and magical.

Just then, Eunice and Pearl arrived with lots of nice things to eat piled on a tray. Unfortunately there weren't any Brussels sprouts, but The Grumpus (nervously to begin with, and then more confidently) tucked into a mug of hot soup, a soft-boiled egg and toast soldiers, then some warm cinnamon rolls fresh from the oven. While they ate, Furball chattered away happily, but The Grumpus was lost in his thoughts. That feeling in his chest was back again, and his brain was feeling a bit itchy too. He realized with astonishment that he wasn't feeling quite as grumpy as he usually did. But how could that be possible? He was sitting in a room in someone else's house that was bursting at the seams with silly Christmas things AND he was eating food that wasn't sprouts. He put a hand to his forehead. Was he poorly? He didn't feel ill, yet he did feel odd . . .

Beside him, Furball yawned. It was time for bed.

Eunice showed The Grumpus and Furball to a small room at the top of the cottage, tucked away under the roof.

'This is lovely,' yawned Furball. 'And it feels just like Christmas Eve, even though it isn't yet – that's tomorrow! All the decorations are up and we've had such nice food.'

'And who knows?' said Pearl as she stood in the doorway, knitting needles in her hand. 'Exciting things might happen in the morning!'

She said goodnight and went down the stairs.

Furball gasped with giddiness at the thought of what the morning might bring, but The Grumpus glowered under the blanket. He was used to things being disappointing and he couldn't see how tomorrow would be different than any other day. The itchy feeling in his chest went away as he remembered that his jumper was ruined and he was now running really late with his Dreadful, Dastardly Plan.

He yawned.

Or did he mean Dastardly, Dreadful Plan? He hadn't thought about it for a few hours now.

He grumpily nestled down further under the blankets, but he jumped when Furball tapped him on the forehead.

'I know it's a secret,' she whispered, 'but you STILL haven't told me why you are going to the North Pole . . .'

The Grumpus froze. What could he say?

Thankfully, he was saved from having to tell her by the sound of little snores that came from her bed.

So The Grumpus lay awake in the darkness, thinking.

At the edge of his hearing he could hear a gentle, regular click-clacking sound. Usually that sort of a noise would have sent him stomping and hollering though the house, but tonight it was oddly relaxing. As he listened he thought about the lights on the tree: the ones he and Furball had put there together. Furball had said one belonged to him. He'd never belonged anywhere before, so did that mean that he was . . . important?

He shook these thoughts from his head and decided to think instead about his Dastardly, Dreadful Plan. He didn't get very far with his think, though, as within a few minutes he had drifted off to sleep.

CHAPTER 15

IN WHICH THE GRUMPUS FINDS HIMSELF STUCK, BUT IN A DIFFERENT WAY THIS TIME

For the second time in as many mornings, The Grumpus opened his eyes to find Furball standing on top of him.

This morning, though, she wasn't brandishing a carrot at him, but was instead dancing on the spot with excitement.

'Wake up! Wake up! Wake up!' she squeaked excitedly.

The Grumpus's head was swimming. Where was he? Why was he in this funny little rooftop room under all these blankets? And what was this annoying little bunny saying to him now? 'HUH?' grunted The Grumpus.

She took his face in her paws. 'It's a new day and that's ALWAYS EXCITING, isn't it?' she cried.

The Grumpus folded his arms and huffed. What a silly thing to say. Every day for The Grumpus was the same, and today wouldn't be any different at all. He thought for a moment, then frowned even more deeply. Actually, today was already worse. He was stuck in the middle of nowhere with an annoying rabbit, his Dastardly, Dreadful Plan was running late, AND – he sighed deeply – his jumper was still ruined. As far as he could see, there was nothing to be excited about at all.

Furball thought differently. She grabbed his hand and tried with all her might to heave him out of the bed. It was like trying to move a mountain. 'Come on!' she cried. 'Let's go downstairs and see what new adventures today will bring!'

The Grumpus tutted, but allowed himself to be hauled across the room by the rabbit. He grabbed hold of The Stick and rolled his eyes in its direction. Then he stumped down the stairs behind Furball, whose fluffy bottom was quivering with joy.

Bright morning light was shining through the cottage windows. It was still snowing outside, but gently now, and in the field around the cottage the sheep were scampering about in their scarves, catching snowflakes on their tongues and baa-ing merrily.

'Good morning!' said Eunice as she came into the room, smiling. She was holding another tray, this time laden with little apple-and-cinnamon buns, still warm from the oven. Pearl followed, carrying a pot of hot chocolate.

Over breakfast, Furball nattered non-stop and at full speed. She was brimming over with giddiness and her nose crinkled often as she threw her head back and giggled with glee. The Grumpus sat beside her like a dark, stormy cloud. He nibbled at the buns and sipped at the hot chocolate. Begrudgingly he had to admit that they were tasty. Not as tasty as Brussels sprouts, but nearly.

The Grumpus looked out of the window at the world outside. If he was going to complete his Dastardly, Dreadful Plan and STOP CHRISTMAS (and he told himself sternly that he WAS going to complete it), he'd have to leave soon. He knew it was going to be a long and cold journey ahead, made colder by his lack of jumper . . .

He wasn't looking forward to leaving at all. The thought of being extra cold made him knit his brows together gloomily.

Suddenly, he felt Pearl pat him gently on the hand. He realized with a flush that she had been talking to him but he hadn't heard her.

He grunted.

'I said,' said Pearl kindly, 'that now we've had our breakfast, I think you'd better look under the Christmas tree.'

Furball looked over the rim of her mug at the tree and her eyes widened. 'The Grumpus!' she gasped.

'There is a parcel there with your name on it!' She grabbed his hand and urged The Grumpus over to the tree, where there was indeed a neatly wrapped parcel under the branches. The Grumpus picked it up suspiciously and looked closely at it. It had his name on it.

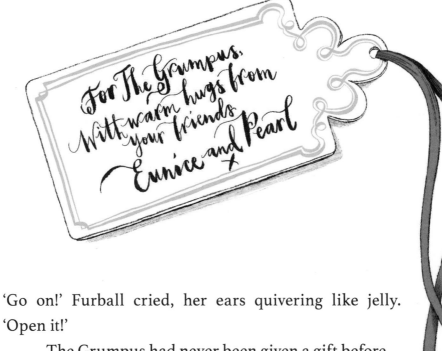

For The Grumpus,
With warm hugs from
your friends
Eunice and Pearl
x

'Go on!' Furball cried, her ears quivering like jelly. 'Open it!'

The Grumpus had never been given a gift before. He'd always thought they were a lot of fuss about nothing, yet here was a present with his name on it! His hands trembled a little bit as he looked at the parcel. He wasn't sure if he wanted to open it. Pearl had wrapped it so carefully and had written his name on it so nicely, he didn't want to spoil it.

'Come on! Come on!' squeaked Furball beside him. 'Open it!'

Feeling a bit embarrassed by the attention, The Grumpus slowly undid the ribbon and opened the parcel up.

His mouth fell open. There, neatly folded on the paper was . . .

'My jumper!' he whispered.

It was no longer a tangle of crinkly yarn, but a jumper again, with a row of Brussels sprouts across the belly.

The Grumpus picked it up and looked at it from all angles. Then, very carefully, he pulled it on. It fitted just as it had before. It felt cosy and comfortable and, he noticed, there were no longer big holes on the elbows. It was beautiful.

The Grumpus discovered that his eyes were prickling. He looked at Eunice, Pearl and Furball, who were all looking at him and beaming. His cheeks went pink and he looked at his toes.

'Thank you,' he said, and he gasped. He'd never said those words before.

'This is JUST like Christmas morning!' squeaked Furball.

The Grumpus frowned. If this is what Christmas morning felt like, then maybe, JUST MAYBE, he'd been missing out on something . . . His heart fluttered

in his chest. He tried his best to look just as stern and disinterested as always, but it was very difficult indeed. The excitement of having his jumper back again made the edges of his mouth twitch slightly, like it wanted to smile.

Beside him, Furball was telling Pearl how clever she was and how smart The Grumpus looked. But The Grumpus wasn't listening. He was lost in his thoughts as he looked down at his belly. Pearl had done this just for him? It was extraordinary. At Christmas, it seemed, people made things and did things for each other, but he couldn't understand why. The Grumpus wanted to think about this more, but he was interrupted by Furball saying, 'FOR ME?'

Pearl had taken another little parcel out from her knitting box and presented it to the rabbit. Pink-cheeked and quivery-eared, Furball opened it. It was a beautiful scarf.

Furball wrapped it around herself and fell over with excitement. 'THANK YOU!' she cried from the rug.

'Well,' said Eunice, 'we couldn't let you leave without a little something, and we hope it will keep you warm on your exciting adventure.'

'Oh!' said The Grumpus. 'Where are you going?'

Furball giggled. 'Oh, you cabbage-head! WE are going to the North Pole, remember?'

It was like someone had suddenly dropped

an icicle down the back of The Grumpus's brand-new jumper.

The North Pole!

His Dastardly, Dreadful Plan!

In the excitement of being reunited with his jumper, he'd quite forgotten his mission. But now an icky feeling was creeping all over him and he wasn't sure why.

He shook his head decisively: he had to set off and soon. He needed to get away from the cottage and Eunice and Pearl, and most of all, Furball. They mustn't know what he'd been planning.

Quickly, The Grumpus grabbed The Stick from where it had been resting by the fireplace, and then he madly began searching for the map.

'No, no,' he grumbled, picking Pearl up and looking underneath her. 'You stay here with your new friends, Furball. I'll be quite all right on my own. Now if I could just find my map . . .'

Furball giggled again. 'But don't you remember? You were so excited to see me last night that you dropped it, and it got whipped away by the wind . . .'

The Grumpus put Pearl down and groaned a great rumbling groan. Pearl's knitting needles rattled in their jar and a cinnamon cake fell off the table. He'd forgotten all about the map being ripped to pieces!

Furball puffed out her chest. 'But don't you worry, I am coming with you!'

'No, you can't!' growled The Grumpus. 'I mean, you mustn't. I mean, I have a Dastardl— I mean, a Very Important Job to do, and I have to do it on my own.'

'But do you know where Father Christmas lives?' asked Furball.

'The North Pole!' said The Grumpus, and Furball giggled again. Eunice and Pearl looked amused.

'But the North Pole is a VERY big place,' she said, kindly. 'I post all our letters from home, so I know Father Christmas's address. It's Mince Pie House, Just Past That Snowdrift, Near the North Pole. And I'm very good at finding things – I found you, and then I found Eunice to rescue you when you were playing in that tree. I will find the right way to the North Pole for you.'

The Grumpus took a deep breath and tried to stay calm, but a little trickle of steam was once again floating out of his earholes. 'I wasn't PLAYING in that tree; I had just fallen off . . .'

He stopped.

Now was not the time.

'I'll . . . I'll just go home instead! Yes – I don't need

to go to see Father Christmas after all!' And he tried to look casual as he picked The Stick up again and sauntered towards the cottage door.

'But you said it was an IMPORTANT JOB that you HAD to do,' said Furball.

The Grumpus groaned again. He was stuck now. She would have to come with him, and he would have to go to the North Pole. There was no point in arguing otherwise.

And so, ten minutes later, The Grumpus found himself waving goodbye to Pearl and Eunice and the sheep while Furball thanked them for their new knitwear and the large hamper of food the shepherdesses had given them for the journey. Then he and the rabbit set off through the snow.

While Furball hummed happily beside him, The Grumpus glowered under his bushy eyebrows. He would have to try and think of a way to shake off this pesky bunny before she found out about his Dastardly, Dreadful Plan.

✛   ✛   ✛

Tools, which had been brought out
to help, lay scattered like fallen
autumn leaves around it.

It was no good. None of them would
fix this problem. This disaster.

It was well past that now.

All they could do was wait.
Hold their breaths and hope that
it didn't get any worse because,
if it did, well . . . well, then
everything would be ruined . . .

CHAPTER 16

IN WHICH THE GRUMPUS IS LED BY SOME WHISKERS AND HIS PLAN IS DISRUPTED FOR A THIRD TIME

Furball took her job as Chief Navigator very seriously indeed.

As The Grumpus trudged through the snow, The Stick in one hand and the picnic hamper in the other, the little rabbit hopped all around him, stopping every so often to listen, think and waggle her ears and whiskers this way and that. She took great sniffs too, from time to time, carefully smelling the air and then pointing the way to go.

Quite how she was finding her way, The Grumpus didn't know. But he didn't really care – he was too busy being a big jumbled ball of feelings.

Firstly, he was grumpy because the snow was thick and cold and difficult to walk through, and the day was freezing and the hamper he was carrying was very heavy.

Then, on top of that, he was cross. Ear-steamingly cross.

'I had a perfectly good idea to STOP Christmas all planned out,' he grumbled quietly to The Stick. 'And now it has been completely bamboozled TWICE!' He stopped to think for a moment, trying to steady himself as Furball led them down an icy hillside into a deep valley, before he continued to grouch and grumble to his twiggy companion. 'And now it is Christmas Eve and I am rushing and huff-puffing through all this stupid snow to get there in time. I should have glued Father Christmas's sleigh to the ground by now and been back home, tutting. If it hadn't been for . . . '

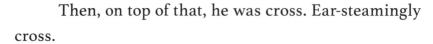

He stopped and glared at the back of Furball, who was bounding about happily, humming Christmas songs, many of which she was making up as she went along.

The Grumpus sighed and huffed. 'How much further?'

Furball, now balancing on a snow-blanketed rock nearby, turned to face him. Mistaking his grumpy pink cheeks for excited rosy ones, she beamed and tumbled over to land neatly by his feet.

'It's exciting, isn't it?' she said, conspiratorially. She hugged his ankle as she fell in step alongside him. 'I can't wait either! I don't think we can be too far away now. Just think of it! The two of us actually at the North Pole! In Father Christmas's Christmassy headquarters!'

She hopped on a few paces, then stopped to waggle her whiskers again. Her ears wiggled too as she rubbed her nose thoughtfully. 'Hmmm . . .' she considered, then she made up her mind with a decisive nod of her head. 'Not far at all. We'll definitely be there by this evening so you can do your Top Secret Very Important Job!'

They carried on lolloping for a few minutes, but The Grumpus could feel the rabbit's eyes on him all the time.

'What?' he grunted.

Furball came and walked right beside him again. 'I was just wondering what your Top Secret Very Important Job is?' she said. 'It must be VERY important indeed for you to go all this way.'

The Grumpus ignored her.

'Oh PLEEEEEEEAAAAASE tell me!' cried Furball. Then she dropped her voice to a whisper. 'I promise I won't tell anyone!' But The Grumpus just grunted and plonked the hamper down on the ground.

'I'm hungry,' he said.

The whole time they chomped their way through their picnic, Furball kept up a steady stream of ideas for what The Grumpus was planning to do once they got to their destination.

'Are you going to deliver a letter?' she said, through a mouthful of carrot sandwich. 'Or help load Father Christmas's sleigh? You must be very strong! Or . . . Or maybe you're going to polish all the reindeer's noses? Or brush Father Christmas's beard for him, so he looks nice and smart?'

She carried on like this for a while, even though The Grumpus didn't answer any of her suggestions. He was still feeling grumpy and cross, but now there was an extra feeling tangled up inside of him. A sour, twisty feeling in his stomach that he was sure was connected to Furball asking all these questions. Why couldn't he just tell her about his Dastardly, Dreadful Plan? Why did the thought of explaining that he was going to the North Pole to STOP CHRISTMAS make him feel . . . What was it? Nervous? She'd be upset, he thought, but why did he care what she felt? He opened his mouth to tell her all about it, but one look at her excited little face made him stop.

Why? He'd never been bothered before about what people thought about him.

Eventually he stood up, brushed the crumbs off his belly and picked up The Stick and the hamper.

'Come on,' he grunted.

The light was fading fast and an icy wind was

getting up. The first few snowflakes of the afternoon were starting to fall, and in the distance the ribbons of dancing coloured lights in the sky were beginning to glow weakly.

Together, The Grumpus and Furball marched on. They marched across snowy fields and frosty lanes. They clambered up hillsides, and slipped and skidded down deep valleys.

'HOW MUCH LONGER?' The Grumpus eventually bellowed, over the now fiercely blowing wind.

Furball stopped her scampering and stood quite still. Her ears twisted, her nose twitched and her whiskers wobbled. Her eyes suddenly grew wide with excitement.

'I think we are almost there!' she cried. 'Quick! Just over this hill!'

The two creatures glanced up at the steep hillside in front of them. It was going to be a tough climb.

They heaved and hauled themselves upward. Furball's excitement at meeting Father Christmas spurred her on, and behind her The Grumpus clambered, grinning to himself that soon he could complete his task and go home. But as they reached the peak of the hill, their hearts sank.

'Oh!' said Furball, flummoxed. 'The sea?' Her brow crinkled.

'The sea!' exclaimed The Grumpus. 'I thought you

were leading us to the North Pole, not taking us to the seaside!'

The Grumpus and Furball looked far below them. At the bottom of the cliff they were now standing on was black churning water, for as far as they could make out. The roaring noise The Grumpus had heard wasn't his grumpiness, but the sound of the waves.

'Oh dear! Oh dear!' cried Furball beside him. 'The North Pole IS just over there –' she pointed towards the horizon, where the ribbons of bright light were flickering in the sky – 'but it seems we'll have to cross the sea to get there!'

The Grumpus let out a great rumbling shout of frustration. 'WE'LL NEVER GET THERE NOW!' he yelled. 'I'VE COME ALL THIS WAY AND—'

But he stopped suddenly. Furball's ears had started to quiver and twist and turn wildly again in the wind.

She'd heard something. Something very exciting indeed.

'We WILL get there!' she hooted, grinning, and she spun and pointed to something behind The Grumpus.

'LOOK!' she said.

CHAPTER 17

IN WHICH THE GRUMPUS FINDS HIMSELF MANHANDLED INTO A BASKET

The dark clouds above the cliffs parted and through them burst a large flock of birds.

Frosty white with icy blue beaks, they majestically cut through the sky, flying at speed, calling to each other with loud, trumpeting honks.

'SNOWBIRDS!' Furball gasped, and as quick as a flash she bounded up The Grumpus until she was standing on his shoulders and began madly waving her arms and shouting.

'What are you doing?' The Grumpus cried.

'Getting us to the North Pole!' said Furball, and for several more moments she continued her shouting and waving.

Eventually one of the birds noticed her, and after honking from overhead, the bird at the front of the flock led them all into a nosedive. They landed, with much wing

flapping and feather fluffing, on the snow-covered cliff.

Up close, the birds were very large, with long necks like geese. Their feathered coats glistened in the moonlight and seemed to sparkle as if they were covered in diamonds. The Grumpus had never seen anything like them before.

There was a flapping in the middle of the flock as the lead bird pushed his way towards The Grumpus and Furball. He was wearing a fancy hat and had medals clipped to his chest feathers.

'I say! What's going on?' he said gruffly. 'Everything all right? Weather's a bit bleak to be out in! Rather strange weather actually, if you must know . . . Very strange indeed. Anyway, shouldn't you both be at home waiting for Father Christmas, eh?'

'You see,' said Furball, 'that's just it. We are trying to get to the North Pole to see Father Christmas. We've got an important something to do – well, he has; I'm just here to help – and we've got to get there before Father Christmas sets off.'

The Grumpus shifted uncomfortably.

'Everything looked like it was going to be a disaster,' she continued, 'but then I heard you all above us and I thought, *We're saved!* You're on your way to the North Pole, aren't you?'

'Yes,' said the Captain. 'Off to meet up with all the rellies like we do every year. Always spend Christmas together, you know. We were going to set off yesterday, but young Geoffrey here couldn't find his hat . . .'

At this, the smallest member of the flock – a fluffy bird only a bit bigger than a chick – shyly stuck his head out from the group and grinned at The Grumpus and Furball. On his head was a bobble hat tied firmly under his chin with a large bow.

'So you're going to the North Pole too, eh?' continued the Captain cheerfully. 'Want us to give you a lift? You'll never sail there in time now. And it doesn't look like you have a boat anyway.'

'Oh, do you mean it?' cried Furball joyfully. 'You'll give us a lift there?'

'Yes, yes, no problem at all,' said the Captain.

The Grumpus couldn't believe it. Here, again, were creatures he'd never met before willing to help. Why would they do that? What special magic did Christmas have that made people behave like this?

The Captain called two of the strongest-looking members of the flock over. 'Hop on the back of Nigel and Gertrude here and we'll get going. Once we get above the clouds, it's actually quite nice flying conditions.'

Furball did as instructed, her face crinkled up with merriment as she settled herself in among Nigel's soft feathers. Then she spotted The Grumpus standing awkwardly beside Gertrude. She was a large bird, but The Grumpus was larger still. He could sit on her back all right, but she wouldn't be able to take off. Suddenly, though, his face brightened.

'It doesn't matter,' said The Grumpus. 'I . . . I can just stay here. Yes, like I said before, Furball, I don't really need to go to the North Pole anyway. I can . . . um . . . just go home.'

Inside, The Grumpus felt like a weight had been lifted.

'Nonsense!' said the Captain, waddling over to investigate. 'Got to get you there somehow. Don't want you to not see your family for Christmas, or whatever. Yeti, are you? Abominable Snowman? All those chaps are up that way, I think.'

The Grumpus didn't say anything, and he tried his best to avoid catching Furball's eye. She was goggling at him quizzically, and he just knew that she was wondering whether he was going to the North Pole to see his family.

'Right!' continued the Captain, clapping his wings together. 'How are we going to solve this conundrum then?'

There was a lot of murmuring as everyone tried to think of a solution. The Grumpus fiddled nervously with the handle of the hamper. What would the creatures around him say if they knew that he was actually going to the North Pole to STOP CHRISTMAS? Suddenly, little Geoffrey pushed forward and whispered something in the Captain's ear.

'Gosh! What a TREMENDOUS idea!' said the Captain. 'Young Geoffrey here says, why don't we use that hamper of yours as a sort of seat, eh? You could sit in there and we'll be able to carry you! Oh, but we haven't any ropes though – you know, to tie to the handle and all that.'

More murmuring, then Furball shouted out with glee, 'What about this?' She pulled her scarf from her neck, took the hamper from The Grumpus and plonked it on the ground. With a little push, The Grumpus found his bottom wedged in it while Furball busily looped the scarf under the handle.

'Now Nigel and Gertrude can have an end of the scarf each!' She beamed.

The Captain laughed. 'Wonderful teamwork, chaps!' he guffawed. 'But, I say, won't you be cold without your muffler?'

'Don't worry,' said Furball. She leaped into the hamper next to The Grumpus and nestled in next to his belly. 'I'll be lovely and warm next to my friend.'

'Oh no, we aren't fr—' The Grumpus started to say, but he stopped. The words wouldn't come out of his mouth.

Furball hadn't heard him as she had been too busy getting herself comfortable, but she noticed his face. 'Don't worry,' she said kindly, mistaking his startled look for anxiety about the flight. 'We'll be all right. Snowbirds are wonderful fliers. Oooh! This is so exciting!'

The Grumpus gulped. He wasn't so sure about that. All around them the snowbirds fussed and preened their feathers as they prepared to take off. Snow was falling quite rapidly now and the Captain was giving instructions to his family. Then, just as they got into position, the moon broke from behind a cloud. It shone brightly, illuminating the snow-covered cliff and the ink-black sea swirling hundreds of feet beneath them.

The Grumpus's heart started to pound in his chest.

One by one the snowbirds spread their wings.

In the hamper, Furball gripped The Grumpus's hand tightly with her tiny paw and then, with a great flapping of wings and a thundering rush, up went the snowbirds. Through the night sky they climbed, and with a sudden jolt the hamper swung up precariously beneath them.

CHAPTER 18

IN WHICH THE GRUMPUS
SEES MANY THINGS ONCE
HE IS ABLE TO OPEN HIS EYES

Higher and higher the snowbirds flew, their wings beating a steady rhythm against the wind. The Grumpus had his eyes squeezed tight shut, but beside him he could feel Furball quivering with excitement.

'THIS IS AMAZING!' she squeaked, her voice barely audible above the rushing air. 'OPEN YOUR EYES! LOOK! YOU'RE MISSING IT ALL!'

But The Grumpus couldn't. He simply couldn't. He was trembling with fear and couldn't, even for a moment, contemplate peeling a finger from The Stick that he was gripping on to or opening an eyelid a fraction.

'Come on!' cried Furball.

The Grumpus felt her warm paw gently squeeze his little finger, and he suddenly felt just a tiny bit braver.

He opened an eye a fraction.

Then he opened the other eye.

Then he gasped.

Furball had been right! This WAS amazing!

Snowflakes were dancing all around them, and above them the snowbirds cut through the dark sky like a cluster of shooting stars.

'Look!' Furball quivered again, tapping his hand and pointing behind them.

The Grumpus's eyes widened to the size of saucers. Below, tiny like a toy, were the snow-covered cliffs they had just left, and there, beyond them, were the hills and valleys they had tramped through that afternoon.

The more he looked, the more he saw. There were the fields they'd crossed. And there . . . was that the teeny, tiny shape of Eunice and Pearl's sheep-like cottage? And was that the woods where he had met Furball and her friends and relations? And could that tiny collection of dots on that mountainside be the town where he lived?

The snowbirds flew on harder, out over the black sea, until all land had disappeared from view. Upward they crept until, with a rush and a sudden burst, they were up above the clouds.

Furball and The Grumpus gazed with amazement as a fluffy landscape spread out below them for as far as they could see.

In the distance, but getting closer, the ribbons of coloured light flickered against the sparkling backdrop of the stars and the moon.

'This . . . this is wonderful!' whispered The Grumpus, and once again Furball squeezed his little finger with excitement.

No sooner had The Grumpus and Furball got used to soaring above the clouds than the snowbirds suddenly nosedived. The Grumpus and Furball yelped in delight as their tummies jumped with the sudden change of direction and the snowy air whipped up all around them.

'We're going to crash into the sea!' cried The Grumpus, gripping on to The Stick with all his might. But right at the last moment the snowbirds pulled themselves upward again, so the hamper with Furball and The Grumpus in it floated just above the waves.

Furball started to laugh with relief, and The Grumpus felt a bubble of giddiness burst in his belly. They reached out their hands and let them gently brush across the surface of the freezing waves that seemed to glow slightly in the moonlight.

Just then, their attention was grabbed by a noise in front of them and they gasped with wonder as a family of whales burst from the depths. They leaped high into the air, twisting and turning in a sparkling shower of water droplets, before plunging into the sea again.

The Grumpus was lost in it all.

He'd had no idea that the world was so big and so

full of wonderful things. He wanted to think carefully about this, but he didn't have the chance. As quickly as they had swooped down to the water, they were up again, high among the clouds. Lights glistened on the horizon in front of them, and it appeared there was even more to see.

CHAPTER 19

IN WHICH THE GRUMPUS HAS A GOOD LOOK THROUGH SOME WINDOWS

Barely a few minutes later, Furball and The Grumpus were flying over land again.

They flew low over tiny towns, where decorated trees stood in town squares, and around them, glowing in the light of the lanterns, people were gathered together, singing.

They passed over buildings with pointy towers, which glowed with the flickering of candlelight, and over people walking home arm in arm through the snow.

Onward they went, the towns becoming bigger, until they were flying down wide, brightly lit avenues.

Everywhere he looked, The Grumpus saw Christmas. Sparkly decorations, lights twinkling, shop windows lit up and piled high with Things.

'Oh isn't it lovely?' Furball sighed.

'All that stuff?' grunted The Grumpus. The jolly

mood the flight had put him in was beginning to disappear. He huffed with annoyance. The towns had all the things he didn't like.

'No,' said Furball. 'Well, yes, but what I mean is . . . ' And she began to point out things that The Grumpus hadn't seen.

Behind all the big sparkles and the twinkles, there were lots of little things to be noticed.

Through each of the windows they flew by, things were happening.

Here were stockings being hung up on fireplaces.

Here were stories being read together.

In some windows people were eating, and in some people were dancing, their bottoms shaking.

In other windows people were singing by decorated trees.

There were loud, busy windows full of parties and excitement.

There were quiet windows where people stood together looking out at the snow.

In some, people stood looking at pictures.

In some there was laughter; in others there was whispering and giddiness.

In some windows there were kisses under mistletoe.

The Grumpus looked at them all, and then he looked at Furball watching them too. Her little face glowed with happiness.

'Christmas!' she whispered. 'It's like a big hug at the end of the year.'

And as the snowbirds swooped up through the clouds again, she settled down next to The Grumpus, nestling in closely to his jumper as they left the city and swooped once again over a wide, black sea.

The Grumpus's head was spinning. He'd always disliked Christmas immensely because of all the stuff – the Things. The stupid sparkly, twinkly, jingly-jangly, crinkly-wrapped-up-with-a-shiny-bow Christmassyness of it all. But now there seemed to be something more to it all . . . What did this mean for his Dastardly, Dreadful Plan?

He huffed. He felt so confused. His chest was tingling, but at the same time his belly felt all twisted like a tangled knot.

Around them the air grew even colder and the night darker, and the snow fell more thickly until the snowbirds were battling through a blizzard. Slowly, they flew lower and lower, until with a skid and a slight bump, they landed on the steep, icy shores of the North Pole.

They had arrived.

The Grumpus forced his eyebrows into a ferocious frown. Maybe if he could complete his Dastardly, Dreadful Plan, it would stop his brain from whirring like it was doing now, and it would put an end to all the strange feelings he had jumbling about inside him. With

Christmas stopped, everything could go back to how it was before. That was when he had understood things – before he had been bamboozled by Furball and Grandma Bear and Eunice and Pearl and the snowbirds.

The Grumpus frowned even more ferociously. Yes, that was what he would do. He HAD to complete his plan.

He had to stop Christmas for good.

And as the wind howled,
and the snow swirled,
it cracked a final crack
and fell apart.

The ground trembled,
and above it the ribbons of
light dancing in the sky
fizzled out once and for all.

CHAPTER 20

IN WHICH THE GRUMPUS DISCOVERS SOMETHING UNUSUAL IN THE SNOW

The wind, thick with snow and fiercely cold, buffeted against the jagged cliffs of the North Pole. Great freezing waves roared against the rocks, and within minutes The Grumpus, Furball and the birds were soaked through.

But it didn't matter, because all around them was joy and excitement as from the steep, icy cliff face came hundreds and hundreds of snowbirds. They hooted and trumpeted. They flapped their wings and hugged and rubbed their beaks together.

'Snowbird kisses!' whispered Furball, delighting in all the fuss and excitement around her. And the snowbirds were excited. After a year apart they had all gathered together to spend Christmas together on the tundra.

'But they haven't got presents for each other,' said

The Grumpus, gruffly. 'I thought Christmas was ALL about presents?'

Furball giggled. 'Oh you really are a silly old turnip!' she said, patting him affectionately on the ankle. 'They ARE the presents to each other. Presents don't have to come in boxes, you know. They are going to spend time with each other and have a lovely time and ooooh it will be wonderful!'

She sighed happily as she wrapped her scarf around her neck. For several minutes, she and The Grumpus watched as the party bounced around them. Then, suddenly, Furball gasped and grabbed hold of The Grumpus, her face a mask of horror.

'What on earth are we doing?' she cried. 'Standing here gawping like we haven't got somewhere important to be!' And she took hold of The Grumpus's ankle and led him through the hooting birds.

Eventually they found the Captain joyfully dancing a high-stepping jig with several of his third cousins twice removed. Furball and The Grumpus were pulled into the dance, and while they were twirled about, Furball tried to talk, but it was useless to try to do anything but prance about with their feathered companions.

'Do you know which way Father Christmas's house is?' she asked urgently, as soon as the dance finished and everyone had paused to catch their breath.

Thankfully, the Captain did know, and he gave

them the instructions they needed. Up the cliff, across the tundra, and soon enough they'd find the Snowdrift. And behind that was Mince Pie House – the home of Father Christmas!

It wasn't terribly far, the Captain explained, but it would be a hard journey. It was getting late and the weather was worsening. Had there not been a blizzard, he and his family would have flown them there, but it was dangerous to fly in this weather, especially above the cliffs.

Finally, he nuzzled his beak against Furball and The Grumpus and wished them luck before the two adventurers set off.

'And Merry Christmas!' he hooted after them.

The Grumpus's tummy twisted at the words.

The Captain had been right – the weather was getting worse and the journey was difficult and dangerous. They gingerly scaled the steep, icy cliff, helping each other over rocks and trying their best not to be blown away by the fierce Arctic wind. Once at the top they paused to catch their breath and to look at where next to go.

Stretching out, seemingly for ever, was snow. Thick, white snow, glowing pale blue in the moonlight and being picked up and thrown about by the blizzard swooshing around them. It was hard to stand upright against the wind, and the two creatures had to brace

against each other to stop from tumbling out to sea. There was, The Grumpus felt, something strange about the scene, but he couldn't quite put his finger on what it was.

Beside him Furball pulled her ears down and used them to shade her eyes from the sheeting snow. She scanned the horizon, then jumped with delight. Her mouth moved but The Grumpus couldn't hear her over the noise, so she pointed wildly and excitedly. He followed her paw and saw it: the Snowdrift.

His stomach dropped and twisted again.

They had to go back. The journey was too dangerous to make in this weather, and what was he going to do when he got to the house behind the wall of snow? He was about to say something when Furball went leaping ahead through the blizzard. She bounded off and then suddenly disappeared. The Grumpus's heart leaped and he ran through the snow, using The Stick to clear the way. He found her completely upside down and stuck in the deep snow. He pulled her out, dusted her off and placed her gently on his shoulders, tutting as he did so. Furball giggled and gripped on tightly to the collar of his jumper.

Out across the tundra The Grumpus stomped, leaning into the wind, each step bringing them closer and closer to the Snowdrift. *At least . . .* thought The Grumpus, concentrating hard to stay up the right way, *we might get some shelter when we get to the house.*

And then, all of a sudden, there they were.

The Snowdrift was vast: a great wall of thick, glistening ice and snow like an enormous wave frozen at full height and arching above them in a curve.

Furball tapped The Grumpus on the head and pointed.

There, almost completely covered by fresh snow, something golden was sticking out. She leaped from his shoulders and struggled across to it. The Grumpus followed, and together they cleared the ice away from it. It was a doorknob! How extraordinary . . .

With a few swipes of his large hands, The Grumpus uncovered the door – it was small and perfectly round, made from thick ice set into the Snowdrift. He pulled it open and, delighted to be out of the blizzard, they tumbled inside to the dark passage beyond.

Under his jumper and his fur, The Grumpus's skin goose-pimpled as he followed Furball down the icy corridor.

'This is so exciting, isn't it!' whispered Furball, but The Grumpus didn't say anything. He felt nervous.

Not only was he worried about what would happen at the end of the passage when he got to Father Christmas's front door, but he also had the strange feeling that something wasn't right at all. He'd felt it from when they'd landed on the shore, and his apprehension had grown as he'd stood on the clifftop looking out across the tundra under the dark, almost black night sky. What was it that was making him shiver with worry? He just couldn't put his finger on it . . .

With a twist, the tunnel arched upward and there was another door. Furball pushed against it and tumbled out. The Grumpus followed, and together they stood looking out at quite a different scene.

The blizzard was still blowing, but now they were in a snow-covered courtyard. In front of them was a collection of large, jolly-looking buildings and a cosy stable block. It was beautiful, but it was also . . .

'Empty,' whispered The Grumpus.

There wasn't a soul about. The Grumpus wasn't sure WHAT he'd expected to find happening at Father Christmas's house on Christmas Eve, but it wasn't this. As he looked around he realized he had expected a scene of bustling busy-ness. Were they too late? Had Father Christmas already taken off into the sky?

There was a noise from the stable block and a reindeer poked his head out, took one look at the blizzard and disappeared from view again. If the reindeer were still here, The Grumpus and Furball realized together, that meant they couldn't have missed the sleigh setting off.

They were still in time!

Furball turned pink with excitement and leaped

across the snow, oblivious to the strangeness of the scene around them. The Grumpus followed, his nervousness growing, and with a few strides he too was at the gigantic front door of Mince Pie House. He gulped as Furball hammered on it. What was he going to say when it was answered? What could he do?

Furball grinned at him, her whiskers quivering with glee.

Suddenly the door creaked open and a tiny figure dressed smartly in a green velvet suit with an apron stood glaring at them.

'Yes?' he said, sternly.

And at the same time, Furball and The Grumpus spoke:

'We are here to help with Christmas!' hooted Furball.

'I'm here to STOP CHRISTMAS!' grunted The Grumpus.

The tiny man looked them up and down.

'Well, you're too late!' he sniffed. 'Christmas has been CANCELLED!'

And he slammed the door shut with a tremendously loud thud.

CHAPTER 21

IN WHICH THINGS
ARE EXPLAINED

'WHAT?' cried Furball and The Grumpus together, staring at the closed door in front of them.

Then Furball turned to The Grumpus.

'What did you say?' she said, her face all shock and horror.

The Grumpus ignored her and instead hammered on the door again.

There was no answer.

He rattled the handle, but it didn't budge. The door was locked!

The Grumpus growled and said a string of rude words ('bum' featured again) before thrusting The Stick into Furball's paws. Then he grabbed the doorknob with both hands and with a quick heave – POP! – the entire door came away from the wall.

The Grumpus tossed the door onto the ground and thundered inside, with Furball racing along behind him.

'What did you just say?' squeaked Furball, her voice, usually so cheerful and excited, sounding tiny now. 'You want to . . .' She gulped. 'You want to stop Christmas?' she whispered. 'But why?'

The Grumpus glanced down at her. Her bottom lip was trembling and her eyes were wide and full of disbelief and sadness.

The Grumpus couldn't face her. He pushed on through the boot room and into a long corridor.

They were now inside Father Christmas's house, but there wasn't time to take in the smell of cinnamon in the air, the strings of children's letters and drawings hung up like fluttering bunting, or the rows of candy-cane coat hooks lining the corridor – The Grumpus and Furball had to find out what was going on.

They burst through the first door they came to and found themselves in a warm, bright workshop. But the scene that greeted them was very glum indeed.

Perched on stools and counter tops and even on shelves sat all of Father Christmas's helpers. They looked worn out and very sad. Many were nursing mugs of hot chocolate. And there, in a large armchair next to the crackling fire, was the man himself.

Father Christmas looked up wearily and squinted

at the new arrivals. 'Oh!' he said softly. '586759, isn't it? I always get your letter in the first bag of post each year . . .' Then he seemed to be struck by how odd it was that a rabbit and a . . . a Something had burst into his kitchen. 'May I ask what you are doing here?'

Furball gathered herself slightly and began talking at nine hundred miles per hour, although not as brightly as usual. 'My name's Furball now and – and we came to help with Christmas – well, SOME of us did,' she said pointedly, wafting her paw as if to say she would explain that later, before breathlessly continuing. 'But what's going on? The person who opened the door said that Christmas has been cancelled! Why? What's happened? Has the sleigh broken? Is there something wrong with the reindeer?'

Father Christmas sighed a deep, heavy sigh. 'No . . . no . . .' he said quietly. 'The sleigh is packed and the reindeer are spruced up and excited. I even have my flask of tea ready . . . But I'm afraid we can't set off. You see –' he sighed again heavily, and then said, in such a sad voice – 'it's broken.'

'What do you mean?' asked Furball. Her whiskers quivered with confusion. Beside her, The Grumpus stood flummoxed by what he was hearing.

Father Christmas got up and pulled back the curtains from the window. The blizzard outside was hurling itself violently against the glass, and the windowpanes were shaking and shivering in their frames. 'Do you see that?' he asked, pointing outside.

It was difficult to see what he was referring to at first. All that could really be seen were thick sheets of snow swirling like a tornado. But the more Furball and The Grumpus squinted, the more they could make something out.

At the top of the hill opposite the house and sticking out from the snow at an awkward angle was the jagged half of a large pole. It was red-and-white-striped like a candy cane, and beside it on the ground, blanketed with thick ice, seemed to be the other half of it. It looked as if it had been snapped in two like an old pencil.

'That's the North Pole itself,' explained Father Christmas. 'Or at least it was. It's been standing tall up there for years – centuries, actually – but a few nights ago it cracked. It was a blizzard that did it. This one tonight is bad, but my goodness, that one was dreadful. If weather had moods, that blizzard would have been the most ferocious tantrum you'd ever have seen! I've never seen anything like it in all the hundreds of years I've been here. As soon as the weather improved we went out and tried desperately to fix it, but – well, you can see for yourself what's happened. And without the North Pole, there is no Christmas.'

The Grumpus knew all about tantrums, of course, but he was struggling to understand what any of this had to do with the big night itself.

'What has a giant old stick got to do with Christmas?' he grumbled.

'It has everything to do with it,' said Father Christmas. 'You see, we are busy here all year round getting ready for Christmas Eve. We read the letters, we make the lists, we build the toys and wrap them up, and we can do all of that perfectly well by ourselves. But on Christmas Eve itself we do need a little bit of assistance to get the reindeer and the sleigh up into the air and around the world all in one night. That's where the North Pole comes in. As soon as the first frost comes, all the fizzy excitement and anticipation for Christmas starts to dance about in the air. You might even have seen it in the skies yourself – the big swirling ribbons of light? THAT'S Christmas magic, and the North Pole draws it all up to us here like a magnet and stores it ready for our big night. Without it, we are stuck. My reindeer and I won't be going anywhere.' He sat down heavily in the armchair.

The Grumpus was busy thinking. So that's what he'd noticed without realizing it – the lights had disappeared from the sky! They'd been flickering all the time on the journey, but he'd been so cross and grumpy or confused along the way that he hadn't noticed. But as he'd stood at the clifftop earlier and looked across the tundra, he'd thought how dark it was all of a sudden. He

141

hadn't realized that the reason it was so dark was because the light show above them had switched itself off.

Beside him, Furball was twittering away in something approaching panic. 'This is awful!' she was squeaking. 'Terrible! Dreadful!'

The Grumpus crouched down and put a hand on her shoulder. 'It doesn't matter,' he said. 'It's only a day. You said earlier that people don't HAVE to have presents—'

Furball shrugged his hand off crossly and looked at him, her face slowly turning a bright beetroot colour.

'But it ISN'T just a day!' she exclaimed, stamping her foot. 'They don't need presents, but this is about MAGIC. All that fizzy excitement that's been in the air! All that giddiness and the looking forward and the loveliness in the air is now lost completely. Everyone will wake up in the morning and it will be like a big burst balloon or . . . or a horrible damp sock!' She glared at The Grumpus really hard. 'You wouldn't understand. YOU came here to STOP CHRISTMAS – I heard you!' she squeaked angrily. 'Well – well . . .'

She stopped, her brain whirring so hard you could practically see it. Then suddenly her whiskers shook and her eyes flashed brightly.

'Well, if no one else is going to fix this mess, I WILL,' she cried. And with a few leaps, she left the house and threw herself out into the blizzard.

CHAPTER 22

In Which There is Much Danger (Oh No!)

The Grumpus, hardly knowing what he was doing, blundered down the corridor and out into the night after her.

The blizzard was fiercer than ever now. Ice and snow whipped all around him in a bitingly cold wind. It was howling so violently it was difficult for him to stand up. Using The Stick to steady himself, he trudged forward, all the time searching through the sheets of falling snow for the rabbit.

'Where IS she?' he growled to The Stick. Worry and panic started to bubble up and pound in his chest. Where had she gone? How could she have vanished so quickly?

And, he wondered, why did he care? Why was he so concerned about her? It had been her choice to go gallivanting about in a dangerous blizzard. It didn't matter to him what happened to her. She was an annoying, chattering little furball who had disturbed his plans, made him fall off a ledge and get tangled in a tree, and had delayed him and made him late in his mission. His Dastardly, Dreadful Plan had been worked out perfectly before she had invited herself along and . . . and changed everything.

'The rabbit is a nuisance!' grumbled The Grumpus, wiping snow from his eyes. And yet, here he was, out in the middle of the night in a snowstorm, frantically searching for her.

And then, slowly, it started to become clear. Furball was an irritating, chattering little ball of fur, and she had done ALL of those annoying things, but she had also helped rescue HIM from that tree. She'd directed him to where he needed to be, she'd found them warmth and shelter, and she'd even managed to get them flown to the North Pole to complete a mission she didn't fully understand. She'd done all of those things because . . . Why?

He thought hard.

Because she was his friend! Yes, that was it – she was his friend! That warm, ticklish feeling that had been tingling on and off in his chest over the past few

days suddenly burst inside of him. It was as warm as hot chocolate and as cosy and as comfortable as his jumper. He realized that for the first time ever he had a friend. That's why he hadn't been able to tell her his plan – he hadn't wanted to upset her: his friend. But now he had made her sad, very sad, and she was in danger. GREAT danger!

He had to rescue her!

The Grumpus scanned the scene in front of him again, desperate for a glimpse of his chum.

Where was she?

But then – right at the top of the hill next to the broken North Pole – there was a flash of colour. It was Furball's scarf fluttering wildly in the wind. The Grumpus pushed and hauled himself up as quickly as he could, using The Stick to help him, until he was beside her. The wind was freezing cold and roaring like a dragon. Furball was pink-cheeked as she pushed and heaved with all her might at the gigantic splintered log.

'FURBALL! IT'S USELESS!' he cried out over the roar and the bluster. 'IT'S BROKEN! WE HAVE TO GET OUT OF THIS STORM!'

But Furball wouldn't listen. Still she pushed and heaved, until The Grumpus put his hand on her and tried to pull her away.

'I HAVE to fix it!' shouted Furball.

'WE CAN'T!' said The Grumpus. 'WE DON'T NEED CHRISTMAS. IT'S ALL SILLY NONSENSE ANYWAY.'

But even as he said it, he knew it wasn't true.

Just then an enormous gust of wind whooshed down the hillside and knocked The Grumpus off his feet.

He tumbled downward, bumping and crashing on his way, only stopping when he managed to get The Stick wedged in the snow. He gripped on to it tightly. It was the only thing stopping him and Furball being torn from the hillside and thrown into the air like glitter in a shaken snow globe.

And there, despite the danger, and despite the awful situation, The Grumpus found himself really thinking hard.

CHAPTER 23

IN WHICH THE GRUMPUS THINKS A LOT OF BIG THOUGHTS VERY QUICKLY

In the blink of an eye, The Grumpus thought an extraordinary amount of thoughts.

Big Thoughts.

His brain whirred like a machine with the memories of the last few days: the paper snowflakes; the warm cottage; the flight across the inky, star-spangled sky. Over and over they went. Then these wispy thoughts started to fly together and connect. Things started to make sense and become clear.

The Grumpus realized that not only had he spent all his life being grumpy and grumbly and cross, he'd also always been afraid. But instead of telling people he was afraid, he had stored up all his worries inside of himself. They'd rumbled and stormed inside him, making him crosser and crosser about everything.

Then, because of all his fearsome grumping and

stomping about, people had become afraid of him. They'd slunk away when he walked by, and in turn he had pulled himself away from them. He had shut himself up tight in his house and had grown grumpier and grumpier, and Christmas had become the focus of his crossness.

At Christmastime, everywhere he looked he saw people having a lovely time, but he felt as if it were a wonderful party that he was looking at through a window from outside; never a part of it. Christmas had become stitched together with all those horribly sad and uncomfortably confused feelings.

I came to glue Father Christmas's sleigh to the ground with treacle, he thought, bewildered at the very idea of it. *But now I don't want to* . . .

He looked down at his silly little friend, who was clinging on to him for dear life, so tiny and tired, but so fiercely brave, and he realized that something had happened to him on this journey to the North Pole.

The journey had changed him.

The Grumpus squeezed his eyes shut, and behind his eyelids danced a vision of his old jumper – tattered and full of holes. Then he saw it unravel and get fixed back together again with the neatly mended row of Brussels sprouts prancing across his belly.

He thought about how it was made from the same old wool it had always been made from, but how that wool had become unravelled. Then, thanks to Pearl's clever knitting, it was fixed! It was the same, but better.

He snapped open his eyes, and a grin – a lovely, happy, jolly, giddy sort of grin – spread across his face. His cheeks glowed pink and the ticklish tingle in his chest wiggled all over him as he realized that that was what had happened to him too!

He had unravelled, but through the fun he'd had with the bunnies, and Grandma Bear's hug, and with Furball's help, and with Eunice and Pearl and all the snowbirds' kindnesses, he had been knitted back together as someone the same, but better.

Kindness.

That was it, he was sure of it – the key to understanding everything, including Christmas. All the jingle-jangle and the twinkle-sparkle of Christmas he'd never liked, he realized, was just the wrapping paper. It was all on the outside. What was inside was the real Christmas.

He suddenly gasped.

Furball was right. Unless the North Pole was fixed, none of that magic would happen and everyone would be bitterly disappointed.

And I will be too! he thought. He'd never had anyone to share Christmas with before, but now he had Furball. Yes, they weren't real family – and, yes, they were very different – but that didn't matter, especially when it came to Christmas. In fact, that's what made it so special!

The excitement of all these sudden thoughts pulled The Grumpus to his senses. With a huge heave, he pulled himself and Furball to safely. He braced himself against The Stick and in a great tumble of words he told her, (well, shouted really, over the wind) all he'd been thinking about.

Furball was perplexed.

Unravelled wool? He was a nicely fixed jumper? She didn't understand a word of it, but The Grumpus's face was lit up and smiling and she found herself giggling with him.

'SO WHAT ARE WE GOING TO DO?' she cried.

The Grumpus gripped The Stick firmly. 'WE ARE GOING TO FIX CHRISTMAS!'

And he knew exactly how he was going to do it.

CHAPTER 24

IN WHICH THE GRUMPUS HAS A NEW PLAN

The Stick had always been The Grumpus's friend. Well, that's how he'd always thought of it, but of course it wasn't a real friend at all. It was simply a stick that he'd grumbled at all the time. Now, having met Furball and Grandma Bear and the Captain and Eunice and Pearl, The Grumpus knew what real friendship was.

Quickly, he explained his plan to Furball. He could see that she was very cold and very tired, but as soon as she heard his idea her eyes sparkled. That determined look she had was back and her whiskers wobbled with excitement.

'It's brilliant!' she cried, and they set to work.

The North Pole was even more of a disaster than it had been before. The large, splintered piece of the Pole was still on the ground covered in a thick coating of ice, but the thundering wind had knocked the remaining piece of the Pole out of the ground and thrown it down into the snow.

The Grumpus bit his lip. The North Pole really was very broken now. Very broken indeed. Was it even fixable?

He shook his head. It HAD to be.

The Grumpus took a deep breath and, using all his strength, he HEEEEAAAAVED and HEEEEEEEEAAAAVED until he had the ends of the two pieces of the broken Pole lined up next to each other on the ground. Furball leaped into action picking up any stray pieces that had splintered off, expertly slotting them back into place like it was a giant jigsaw.

It was terribly hard work. The blizzard was raging around the two adventurers, threatening to hurl a piece of the Pole across the frozen tundra at any moment. Several times an icy blast almost sent them flying, but The Grumpus kept a firm hold on the Pole and made sure Furball was safe too. By working together, they had soon got all the pieces of broken wood back in place and the crack had almost entirely disappeared.

When they were satisfied that everything was right, The Grumpus handed Furball The Stick and she pressed it to the side of the Pole. Then, very carefully, she unwrapped her scarf from her neck and wound it tightly around The Stick and the Pole, bracing them together and making the Pole strong again.

The Grumpus took one end of the scarf, and Furball took the other, and they pulled it tight like a bandage around everything that had been broken.

They looked at each other.

Would this work?

What would happen if it did?

And (a grim thought) what would happen if it didn't?

They both swallowed hard. They knew they had to try.

Carefully, The Grumpus picked up the mended North Pole, bracing himself against the wind and hoping that a great gust wouldn't come and shatter it all over again. The Stick and the scarf were doing their job and, although it wiggled this way and that, the Pole was staying in place. It was terrifically heavy though. The Grumpus's face went red and beads of sweat appeared on his brow.

With a leap, Furball jumped onto his shoulders and, clasping the Pole with her paws, she helped as best she could. Around them the blizzard screamed.

'Ready?' grunted The Grumpus.

'Ready!' cried Furball.

They squeezed their eyes shut.

They counted to three.

One.

Two.

Three.

Then – THUMP!

They plunged the North Pole back into the ground.

CHAPTER 25

IN WHICH THERE IS MAGIC

Even the wind and the snow had stopped. All was still. Eerily still.

And then, far beneath their feet, deep below the snow and the earth, there came a deep, deep rumbling.

The ground shook.

The Grumpus and Furball held their breaths.

Then – BANG!

An explosion! An enormous, magical explosion!

The Grumpus felt himself being thrown up into the air, but then, curiously, he didn't feel himself falling back down to earth.

His heart was pounding and he was breathing hard. Suddenly he felt a tapping on his hand and then heard Furball's voice in his ear.

'Open your eyes, you silly parsnip!' She laughed. 'Look at it all! It's . . . It's . . .'

She sighed deeply and The Grumpus slowly opened his eyes and looked around him.

'It's WONDERFUL!' he gasped. And it was.

He was barely able to comprehend what he was seeing. He couldn't even tell where he and Furball were! They were floating in mid-air! The magic bursting from the fixed North Pole was so great, it had sent The Grumpus and Furball flying upward until they were swimming through the clouds.

The sky all around them was illuminated and sparkling. The ribbons of light had returned, shimmering and swirling, but somehow they were now brighter and more brilliant than ever before. Pulsing pinks and flashing greens, bouncing blues and rippling oranges, flashes of purple and silver and starlight.

But there was more! Images appeared, seemingly made from starlight and magic: snowflakes, both real and paper, danced around them. Furball's ears twisted about as the sound of bells jingle-jangling drifted on the wind. Loud peals of laughter joined in, followed by the soft sound of stories being shared and the lovely twinkling sound of music and singing too. It all knitted together like an orchestra playing something wonderful and very beautiful.

The Grumpus and Furball listened to it all and gazed in amazement. Suddenly, like fireworks sparkling in the sky, there appeared all sorts of things prancing and swishing through the night. Stars and sparks of magic flashed and formed glittering pictures of ribbons and

tinsel, great bunches of holly and mistletoe, glowing lanterns, sugar plums, cookies and, yes – The Grumpus could hardly believe it – even Brussels sprouts!

Twisting and turning through all of this was the smell of gingerbread, cinnamon, the crisp, crackly smell of frost, and then the warm, cosy smell of a glowing fire.

The Grumpus and Furball gasped in amazement as they bobbed about watching it all. Then, slowly and very gently, they landed back down on to the ground. The blizzard had stopped, and the sky was clear and glowing with the magical light.

There was a sound from behind them and the two friends turned to see Father Christmas and his helpers streaming out from the house. They cheered and clapped and danced and hugged. Father Christmas squeezed The Grumpus and Furball tightly as his beard wobbled with glee.

'You did it!' he cried. 'You fixed it! Oh how clever you both are!'

Then, putting them down again, he snatched a watch on a chain out from his pocket and looked at it. 'We aren't too late!' he hooted. 'We still have time! There's still time to deliver Christmas!'

CHAPTER 26

In Which The Grumpus Learns Something Interesting About Treacle

Everything that happened in the next half an hour happened in a complete blur of action and excitement. The Grumpus and Furball followed Father Christmas and his gang down the hill, and they all got to work.

The Grumpus helped clear the sleigh of all the fresh snow that had fallen on it. All of the helpers bustled about making sure the enormous sacks full of gifts were securely fastened. Furball led the reindeer out and got them hitched up, and then, with a fresh flask of tea tucked into his belt, Father Christmas announced that all was ready. He asked whether The Grumpus and Furball wouldn't mind joining him in the sleigh and helping him to deliver all the presents. He could deliver them back to their homes before morning.

'REALLY?' gasped Furball, her eyes enormous

with excitement. 'You really mean it? I get to ride in Father Christmas's sleigh?' She hugged Father Christmas's knees and bounded into the sleigh, pulling The Grumpus with her.

And then they were off! Up into the sky again, flying through the clouds and marvelling at everything that whizzed below them.

It was a long and busy night. Together with Father Christmas, they helped deliver presents to every house and every home on the list, helped, of course, by the Christmas magic floating in the air from the North Pole.

Eventually the dark night sky started to lighten a little. The magical lights began to fade, and morning was on its way. Furball, exhausted from the excitement of the evening, slept soundly next to The Grumpus, smiling as she snored.

The Grumpus was tired too, and still glowing with that ticklish, tingly warm and Christmassy feeling, but there was a little Something niggling at him. Something he felt he had to do.

Shyly, he told Father Christmas all about his journey to the North Pole and even about his Dastardly, Dreadful Plan. Then he told him everything he had realized when he had been stuck out in the blizzard.

'Ah . . .' said Father Christmas, nodding as he finished listening. 'I did wonder about that. I heard that you had come to stop Christmas and I wondered what had changed your mind.'

'I'm sorry,' said The Grumpus, and he was surprised to see Father Christmas smiling.

'It's all right,' Father Christmas said kindly. 'It's never too late to change and be mended – just look how you fixed the North Pole. I thought that Christmas could never happen again, and yet you fixed it all beautifully.' Then Father Christmas suddenly laughed. 'And besides, you couldn't have stuck my sleigh to the ground with treacle, because there isn't a single pot of it at my house! I can't stand the stuff – so sticky!' And he shuddered at the thought.

The Grumpus laughed. Then he laughed louder as he realized that he had never, ever laughed before. It felt good, like magic bubbles dancing inside him.

'Now,' said Father Christmas, 'I'll drop you at your house and take little Furball here home on my way back up north. Is that OK?'

The Grumpus nodded, and then suddenly started. No, he couldn't go straight home! There was one more job he needed to do.

CHAPTER 27

IN WHICH THE GRUMPUS DOES THINGS

Everything that happened in the next half an hour happened in a complete blur of action and excitement. The Grumpus and Furball followed Father Christmas and his gang down the hill, and they all got to work.

The main square was deserted when The Grumpus set foot upon it. He waved goodbye to Father Christmas and when the sleigh had disappeared again into the sky, he shivered. In his hand was a large sack containing the presents for the people of his town. But before he could deliver them, The Grumpus had something to do.

He looked about. All around him was untidiness. The mess he had made in that ferocious grump he'd been in when he had left his town all those days ago hadn't been fixed, and he wasn't surprised. There was so much it! Strings of lights hung untidily from buildings, swags of holly lay tattered on the ground, and the large

Christmas tree was still on the floor where he'd pushed it, surrounded by fallen baubles.

The Grumpus sighed. He couldn't believe how grumpy he had been!

'But now I need to fix it,' he said, and so he carefully began putting everything back where it should be. He fixed the lights and lit the lanterns. He mended the holly swags and rehung them as best he could. He was so busy with his tasks that at first he didn't notice that he was being watched.

Slowly, the town had woken up, probably stirred by the noises coming from The Grumpus working in the town square. They weren't grumpy noises, but whistling. The Grumpus was actually whistling, and he was whistling Christmas songs too!

Faces appeared at windows.

Could that really be . . . ? Was it . . . ?

It was!

So amazed were they by what they were seeing, they forgot about the fact that there didn't seem to be any presents under their trees. They were too busy goggling to notice that the stockings hung around their fireplaces with care were completely empty.

Out they came, tiptoeing across the snow in their slippers to gather around, eyes like dinner plates, watching as The Grumpus continued to work.

He didn't look at them. He was shy and worried

about what they might say, so he concentrated on righting the tree again in the centre of the town. Then, when that was done, he reached down to collect the first bauble, but was surprised to find it being handed to him.

It was a mouse – the one who had bought the very last sprout from Frau Butternut's shop! She'd crept across the snowy square and was now handing him the bauble.

He took it from her with a smile and gently placed it on the tree. The mouse nodded approvingly at the placement of it. She helped The Grumpus with the other decorations, and before long the tree was looking festive and lovely again.

Then, after a night when many extraordinary things happened, something else happened.

Remembering the sackful of gifts Father Christmas had asked him to deliver, The Grumpus began handing them out. But to his surprise, not one person opened them. Instead, they all looked at him – really looked at him. It was as if they were just at that moment seeing him for the first time. And then, one after another, they wrapped their arms around him and they hugged him, until The Grumpus found that he was in the middle of a giant Christmas-morning hug.

And he hugged them back.

✥ ✥ ✥

A few hours later, after The Grumpus had spent some time getting to know the people of his town, he yawned extravagantly. He hadn't realized quite how tired he was, and he decided it was time to go home and have a sleep. He waved goodbye to all his new friends and started to slump off back up the hill to his house.

It had been a lovely morning, but he couldn't help feeling strange. It would be odd to be on his own again after all his adventures. Sleepily, as he opened his door, he thought about Furball and how excited she would be waking up with all her friends and relations. He hoped she was having a nice morning.

Suddenly, he prickled.

In the dark of his house, he'd heard a noise!

He listened.

Yes, there it was again.

He'd definitely heard something. He scrabbled around for his lantern and lit it.

'Well, where have YOU been, you silly turnip?' said a voice.

He spun around and gasped.

There was Furball, sitting on his kitchen table, giggling. 'Father Christmas dropped me off here AGES ago!' She laugh-snorted.

The Grumpus picked her up and squeezed her tightly. She laughed again and hugged him back before remembering something. The Grumpus put her down and from a bag she pulled out a present.

'For you!' she said, and she handed it to her friend.

The Grumpus took it, hardly daring to believe that here in his hand was his very first proper Christmas-morning present.

'Well open it then!' squeaked Furball excitedly.

He did and he smiled.

It was what he'd always wanted all along.

It was a great big bowl of Brussels sprouts.

Now I know that you know about The Grumpus.

And about his friend, the rabbit called Furball.

*And about the Wonderful Thing that happened on
Christmas Eve when things that were broken were mended.*

But do you know what happened after that?

About what happened the following winter?

Perhaps I should tell you about it . . .

EPILOGUE

IN WHICH IT IS
ALMOST A YEAR LATER

Once upon a winter's morning, The Grumpus stood in the door of his house, scratching his armpit with a fork.

There was a crisp, crackly coating of frost on the ground. Everything was white and twinkly and crunchy as far as The Grumpus could see. There was also a chill in air, a shiver, and just fading from sight as the weak sun rose were the last faint traces of the magical Christmas lights dancing across the morning sky.

The Grumpus took it all in. He knew exactly what it all meant. What it all added up to . . .

Suddenly there was a voice. 'Stop looking so grumpy, you turnip!' it said, cheerfully. 'It was YOUR idea to set off this early in the morning!' And from behind the trees came Furball, pink-cheeked and with supplies for the journey.

The Grumpus brightened immediately at seeing

his friend. 'I'm not grumpy!' he said. 'I was just worried you weren't coming!'

Furball pretended to be shocked. 'And miss our special adventure?' she said. 'I don't think so!'

The Grumpus grinned. He was feeling all wiggly with excitement.

'Have you remembered the plan?' asked Furball.

'Of course!' said The Grumpus, pulling a piece of paper out from under his jumper. 'But I know it off by heart anyway. Shall I read it to you?'

Furball nodded and The Grumpus cleared his throat. 'Furball and The Grumpus's VERY Special Christmas Adventure Plan,' he read.

He stopped for a moment for effect, then continued:

'Number One: Visit the Burrow and have a pretend-snow day with Grandma Bear and all of Furball's friends and relations.

'Number Two: Call in on Eunice and Pearl to say hello to the sheep. Help decorate their house and pick up a new pair of socks.

'Number Three: Meet the Captain and his family and fly to the North Pole.

'Number Four: Arrive at the North Pole, give the socks to Father Christmas and help get everything ready for Christmas.'

He looked at Furball. Her whiskers were wobbling

with glee. 'Have I missed anything?' he asked.

'No,' said Furball, and she sighed. 'It's perfect!'

The Grumpus nodded. He completely agreed.

And with that, the two friends set off down the frosty lane together.

And it was lovely.

THE END

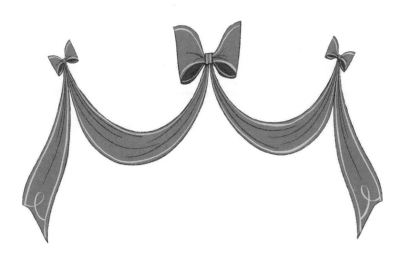

HAVE A VERY JOLLY CHRISTMAS WITH
ALEX T. SMITH

This book is for
Max and Rory and their very special Grumpa, Peter

First published 2022 by Macmillan Children's Books
an imprint of Pan Macmillan
The Smithson, 6-9 Briset Street, London, EC1M 5NR
EU representative: Macmillan Publishers Ireland Limited, 1st Floor,
The Liffey Trust Centre, 117-126 Sheriff Street Upper, Dublin 1 D01 YC43
Associated companies throughout the world
www.panmacmillan.com

ISBN 978-1-5290-4161-3

Text copyright and illustrations © Alex T. Smith 2022

The right of Alex T. Smith to be identified as the author and illustrator of this
work has been asserted by him in accordance with the Copyright, Designs and
Patents Act 1988.

1 3 5 7 9 8 6 4 2

A CIP catalogue record for this book is available from the British Library.

Design by Alison Still

Printed and bound in China

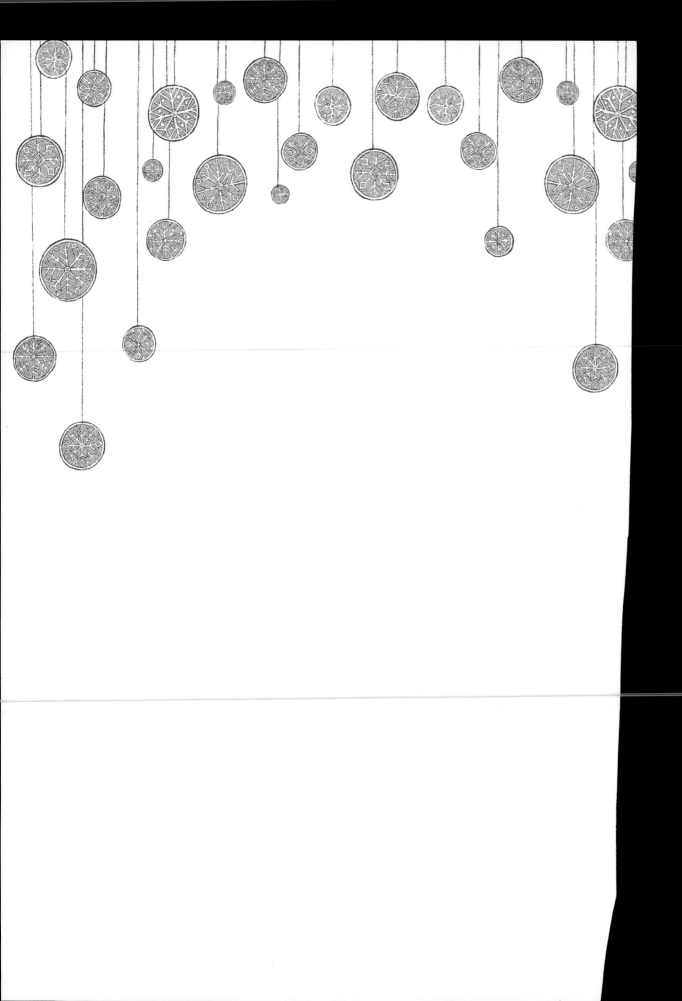